A DEBT PAID
IN THE
MARRIAGE BED

A DEBT PAID IN THE MARRIAGE BED

BY

JENNIFER HAYWARD

MILLS & BOON

First published in Great Britain 2017
By Mills & Boon, an imprint of HarperCollins*Publishers*
1 London Bridge Street, London, SE1 9GF

Large Print edition 2017

© 2017 Jennifer Drogell

ISBN: 978-0-263-07113-9

Printed and bound in Great Britain
by CPI Antony Rowe, Chippenham, Wiltshire

For my dad—a gifted surgeon, teacher, woodworker and master of anything trivia, you were also the greatest father I could have hoped to have.

There is a piece of you, Dad, in every hero I write, because you were larger than life. I can't imagine a world without you, where I can't ever pick up the phone again and pick your brain on a storyline. I only know if I live a life half as courageous and remarkable as yours I will be happy. xx

CHAPTER ONE

"Sir."

Lorenzo Ricci pocketed his phone and lengthened his stride, pretending he hadn't witnessed the appearance of his portly, balding, middle-aged lawyer in the hallway behind him. Fifty minutes back on US soil, the last thing he needed was to discuss the fine print of the complex acquisition deal he had been negotiating, a subject bound to make his head ache even more than it already was.

Tomorrow, after a shot of his favorite whiskey, a steam shower and a face-plant into the Egyptian cotton sheets his housekeeper had procured for his very comfortable king-size bed, would be soon enough to endure that brain-throbbing task.

"Sir!"

Dio. He pulled to a halt, turned and faced the man doing his best to catch up to him on short, stubby legs, his outward appearance the very antithesis of the pit bull he was in the boardroom.

"I've been traveling for sixteen hours, Cristopher, I'm tired, I'm in a vile mood and I need sleep. Trust me when I say tomorrow is better."

"It can't wait." The edge to his lawyer's voice commanded Lorenzo's full attention. Not once in five years of completing difficult and sometimes downright antagonistic deals together had his legal counsel ever looked this rattled. "I need five minutes of your time."

Expelling a long sigh, his stomach souring at the thought of attempting to interpret the finer points of legalese when what his brain officially needed was sleep, Lorenzo waved a hand toward his office. "*Bene.* Five minutes."

Cristopher followed him into the sleek, black-and-chrome offices of the Ricci International executive team. Gillian, Lorenzo's ultraefficient PA, gave him an apologetic I-tried look. He waved her off. "Go home. We can go through everything in the morning."

She murmured her thanks, got to her feet and started gathering her things. Cristopher followed him into his office, hovering in front of his desk while he dropped his briefcase beside it and shrugged off his jacket. The apprehension skittering up his spine deepened. His lawyer didn't hover. *Ever.*

He walked to the bank of floor-to-ceiling windows framing a magnificent view of a dusky, indigo-lit Manhattan—one of the perks of being CEO of his family's international Italian conglomerate, a shipping dynasty he had evolved into a diverse empire that included hotel chains, cruise lines and real estate arms. He loved the view, but tonight, it barely penetrated the fatigue clouding his brain.

Turning, he leaned back against the glass and crossed his arms over his chest. "All right," he said, "give it to me."

His lawyer blinked behind gold-rimmed spectacles, flicked his tongue over his lips and cleared his throat. "We have a…situation. A *mistake* that's been made we need to rectify."

He frowned. "On the deal?"

"No. It's a personal matter."

Lorenzo narrowed his gaze. "I didn't invite you in here to play twenty questions, Cris. Spit it out."

His lawyer swallowed. "The legal firm that handled your divorce made an error with the filing of the papers. An *omission*, actually…"

"What kind of an omission?"

"They forgot to file them."

A buzzing sound filled his ears. "I divorced my wife *two years ago.*"

"Yes, well, you see…" Another long swallow. "You didn't actually. Not in the technical tense because the papers were never filed with the state."

The buzzing sound in his head intensified. "What are you saying?" He asked the question slowly, deliberately, as if his brain was having trouble keeping up. "Just so we're clear?"

"You're still married to Angelina." Cristopher blurted the words out, a hand coming up to resettle his glasses higher on his nose. "The lawyer who handled your divorce had an insane caseload that month. He thought he'd asked his clerk to file the papers, was sure he had, until we went back to look at the specifics after the conversation you and I had recently."

When it had become clear Angie was never going to touch a penny of the alimony he gave her each month.

"My wife announced her engagement this week. To *another man.*"

The lawyer pressed a hand to his temple. "Yes…

I saw the piece in the paper. That's why I've been trying to track you down. It's a rather complicated situation."

"Complicated?" Lorenzo slung the word across the room with the force of a bullet. "How much do we pay that firm an hour? Hundreds? Thousands? To *not* make mistakes like this. *Ever.*"

"It's not acceptable," Cristopher agreed quietly, "but it is the reality."

His lawyer squared his shoulders, looking ready to be verbally flogged to within an inch of his life, but Lorenzo had lost the power of speech. That his short-lived marriage to his wife, a disaster by its ignominious end, had, in fact, never been legally terminated was too much to take when heaped upon the other news his father had delivered today.

He counted to ten in his head, harnessing the red-hot fury that engulfed him. *This* he did not need as he attempted to close the biggest deal of his life.

"How do we fix this?" he asked icily.

Cristopher spread his hands wide. "There are no magical solutions. The best we can do is hope to expedite the process. But it could take months. It will still mean— I mean you'll still have to—"

"Tell my wife she can't marry her boyfriend so she doesn't commit *bigamy*?"

His lawyer rubbed a palm across his forehead. "Yes."

And wouldn't that be fun, given Angelina was set to celebrate that engagement in front of half of New York tomorrow night?

He turned to face the jaw-dropping view, blood pounding against his temple in a dull roar. He was shocked at how much the idea of Angie marrying another man repulsed him even though he had once convinced himself if he never saw his wife again it would be too soon. Perhaps because her vibrant, sensual, Lauren Bacall-style beauty haunted him every time he thought about taking another woman to bed… Because every time he tried to convince himself he was ambivalent about her, he failed miserably.

The conversation he'd had with his father before leaving Milan filtered through his head like some sort of cruel joke, had it not been of an entirely serious nature. The chairman of Ricci International had fixed his impenetrable, ice-blue stare on him and dropped a bombshell. "Your brother Franco is unable to produce an heir, which means it's up to you, Lorenzo, to produce one and produce it soon."

His dismay for his younger brother, his bewilderment Franco hadn't told him this the night before over dinner, had evaporated under the impact of his father's directive. *Him marry again?* Never happening. Except, he conceded with bitter irony, he was apparently *still* married. To the woman who had walked out on him and said he had no capacity to love. The woman who had stolen the last piece of humanity he'd possessed.

"Sir?"

He turned around. "Do you have any more bombshells to add to the pile or is that it?"

"That's it. The deal is fine for the moment. We're still negotiating the smaller points and you need to clear those last couple of tricky items with Bavaro, but other than that we're on track."

"Bene." He waved a hand toward the door. "Go. I'll take care of Angie."

His lawyer nodded. "Do you want me to file the papers? Get the process started?"

"No."

Cristopher gave him a stupefied look. "Sorry?"

"*I said* leave it."

His lawyer left. A wise decision. He walked to the bar and poured himself a whiskey. Padding back to the windows, he lifted the glass to his mouth and took a sip. Began to feel vaguely human as the spirit warmed his insides and smoothed out the raw edges—raw edges that had been festering ever since one of the clippings in his daily press briefing had buzzed about his former wife...*current* wife's betrothal plans to a prominent Manhattan lawyer.

He had pushed the news of Angie's engagement aside. Refused to acknowledge how it sank its claws into his skin, dug into his insides—inspired dark, inexplicable thoughts he couldn't have identified if he'd tried. Angie had ended a marriage that had descended to the very deepest depths of acrimony, a marriage many would have left for dead. So why did it still sting so much?

Why was he still so angry, still so damn angry it was like a disease inside of him, eating away at his soul? He *itched* he was so angry.

Why hadn't he asked Cris to file those papers?

Ended something that should have been ended two years ago?

He stared out the window for a long time, sipping the whiskey, watching night fall over a light-strewn Manhattan. Considered his duty to the Ricci line. The fifteen-billion-dollar acquisition deal in front of him—a deal that required every bit of his concentration—that would make Ricci the top luxury hotel chain in the world if he landed it.

The solution to his predicament, when it came, was shockingly, simplistically clear.

Why wasn't there any air in this room?

Angie took the glass of champagne the bartender handed her, turned and leaned against the lit glass surface, surveying the cocktail-dress-attired crowd mingling in the elegant, white-washed art-gallery space. Shimmering light from the antique chandeliers cascaded onto gleaming black marble floors, while directed lighting spotlighted the stunning artwork on the walls. A perfect, sophisticated backdrop for her and Byron's engagement party, everything they'd envisioned to celebrate their upcoming nuptials. Why then did the room seem to have drained of oxygen as the night wore on? Why this restless pull in her veins she couldn't explain?

She *should* be ecstatic. She had the career of her dreams as one of New York's most buzzed-about new jewelry designers, the freedom she'd always craved from life as a Carmichael and a wonderful man waiting in the wings. What more could she ask for?

And yet something still felt…missing.

It did not, she told herself firmly, have anything to do with the man who haunted the edges of her happiness. Who had shown her what having everything looked like, then taken it away in the next breath. Because she knew now that kind of an adrenaline rush was for fools. What went up must come down, and in her and Lorenzo's case, had come crashing down.

A searing pang throbbed in her chest. She took a deep breath of the nonexistent air. Perhaps that's what she needed—oxygen to clear her head.

Byron engaged with a business colleague across the room, she seized the moment. Winding her way through the buzzing crowd, around the live jazz band to the elegant staircase that led to the second level, unused tonight, she climbed the stairs and headed for the small terrace that opened off the upper level.

Hot, thick summer air hit her like a wall of heat as she stepped outside. She walked to the edge of the beautifully landscaped space, rested her elbows on the railing and drank it in. The frenetic activity in the street below as cabs and pedestrians battled for supremacy on a sticky Manhattan night was a familiar refrain that soothed her senses.

Another sensory impression seeped in. Spicy, masculine, it was imminently familiar. *Disturbingly, distantly familiar.*

Cold fingers clamped down on her spine. Her heart a drumbeat in her throat, she turned around. Her brain flatlined as she took in the tall, dark-haired, olive-skinned male dressed in an exquisitely tailored suit standing in front of her. She lifted her gaze to his hard, dark eyes, as treacherous as black ice. Moved them down over Lorenzo's prominent Roman nose, the day-old stubble lining his jaw, his beautiful, sensual mouth that knew how to wound and pleasure in equal measure.

For a disturbingly real second or two, she thought she'd conjured him up. That he wasn't actually here, but was a product of the strange, restless mood she was in. That, in this fantasy of hers, he'd heard about her engagement and come here to stop it. That he still cared about her, because once, during the stormy complexity of their marriage, she'd sworn he had.

A panicked pulse echoed through her. What if he had? What would her answer be? She was terrified she'd cave like a ton of bricks.

She pressed her champagne glass to her chest before her shaking hands spilled it. Before she allowed herself to start conjuring up the fairy tales she'd always had about this man. That maybe he'd wanted *her* when he'd married her. That what they'd had in the beginning *had* been magic, instead of the reality that had materialized like a harsh slap to the face.

That he had married her for political expediency, to secure his heir, and when she'd lost their baby he'd lost all interest in her. *Shattered her.*

She took a deep breath, shifted her weight to both feet in an attempt to gain some equilibrium. "What are you doing here, Lorenzo?"

His lethally handsome face twisted in a mocking look. "No 'Hello, Lorenzo'...? 'You look well, Lorenzo'...or even a 'How are you, Lorenzo?'"

Her mouth tightened. "You've crashed my engagement party. I hardly think pleasantries are in order. We abandoned those at about month six of our marriage."

"Did we last that long?" He crossed his arms over his chest and leaned back against the railing. She forced herself not to follow the ripple of muscle in that powerful body. To acknowledge how he seemed to have hardened into an even more dangerously attractive version of the man she'd known.

He lifted a shoulder. "My apologies for showing up out of the blue, but I have business we need to discuss."

"Business?" She frowned. "Couldn't we have discussed it over the phone?" She flicked a nervous glance toward the door. "Did Byron—"

"No one saw me. I blended in with the paint. I did get a chance to listen to the speeches, though. Touching as they were."

She stared at him, horrified. "How long have you been here?"

"Long enough to see you clearly have *Byron* roped and tied, as my rancher friend, Bartlett, would say. Fully enamored with your considerable charms…ready to let you run the show. Is it everything you ever dreamed of, Angie?"

Her blood heated, mixing with the panic fizzling her veins. "I never wanted to run the show. I wanted equal billing in our relationship—something you, in your arrogance and chauvinism, refused to give me."

"And our good friend Byron does?"

"Yes."

"What about in bed?" His eyes glittered with deliberate intent. "Does he satisfy that insatiable appetite of yours? Does he make you scream when you wrap those long legs of yours around him and beg? Because he doesn't look *man* enough to me, *cara*, to deliver it the way I know you like it. Not even close."

Lust slammed into her hot and hard. An image of Lorenzo's beautiful, muscular body imprinted itself on her brain, filling her, pushing her to the limits of her pleasure, his voice a hot whisper at her ear, demanding she tell him if it was good, not satisfied until she'd begged to let him know it was, until she'd screamed, because yes, he *had* made her scream.

Blood rushed to her cheeks, her stomach contracting in a heated pull. She'd been so desperate for his love, for his affection, she'd taken whatever crumb he'd been willing to throw at her. In the end it had been all they'd had.

She sank her teeth into her bottom lip. Lied. "I have no complaints in that area, either."

His eyes hardened, a dark glimmer stealing across their ebony depths. "Too bad it just isn't going to work out."

A frisson of apprehension swept through her. "What are you talking about?"

"Well, you see, there's been a…hiccup in the paperwork for our divorce."

"We *are* divorced."

"So I thought. The firm handling the paperwork failed to file the correct papers with the state. The error was brought to my attention yesterday after I asked them to review the document."

Her knees went weak. "What are you saying?"

"We're still married, Angie."

The floor gave way beneath her feet. She grasped the railing, wrapping her fingers around cool metal to steady herself. Blinked as she tried to work through the fog enveloping her brain. *Married?* She and Lorenzo were still married?

She swallowed past a paper-dry throat. "I'm marrying Byron in three weeks...in St. Bart's. We're eloping."

His stare was bold, aggressive, like the predator he was. "Unless you plan on committing *bigamy* that would be impossible."

She struggled to get her brain in working order. "You need to *do* something. *Fix* this. It's your firm's fault. *They* should fix it."

An indolent shrug. "There's only so much they can do. These things move at a snail's pace. It could take months to push it through."

"But you *know* people. You have influence in all the right places...you could make it happen."

"Perhaps."

Her blood ran cold at the hard, unforgiving lines of his face. "But you don't plan to use it."

"No. It would be an unnecessary calling in of favors."

Unnecessary? A red mist descended over her vision. "I am getting *married* in three weeks. It's all planned. How is that *unnecessary*?" She shook her head, pinned her gaze on his. "Are you still angry with me? Is that it? You want to punish me for walking out on you? For God's sake, Lorenzo, you knew our marriage was doomed. You knew it was never going to work. Let me move on."

He stepped closer, six foot three inches of far too intense male vibrating just centimeters from her. His expression, when he looked down at her, was full of leashed aggression. "Our marriage was not *doomed*. Our marriage failed because you were too young and selfish to realize that marriages take work. *Effort*, Angelina. Instead you put all your energy into rebelling against what I asked of you. Into ignoring what *I* needed."

She lifted her chin. "You wanted a perfect society wife without a mind, a *purpose* of her own. You should have hired a beautiful robot to fill the role. It would have been the perfect match for you."

His eyes flashed. "Don't be sarcastic, *cara*, it doesn't suit you. I liked your mind, you're well aware of that. I offered you all sorts of chances to get involved in the charitable efforts Ricci supports, but you didn't have any interest in them, no matter how challenging." He pointed his glass at her. "As for being my society wife, you knew what you were getting into when you married me. What the reality of my life was."

Had she really? Twenty-two, pregnant and wildly infatuated with her husband, she'd had no idea she'd been exchanging one lonely existence for another. That instead of finding the love she'd craved, she'd be giving up the very independence she'd been searching for, the dreams she'd had of being a jewelry designer. That she'd be following in her mother's footsteps in falling for a man who had no capacity to love—the one mistake she'd sworn never to make.

She lifted her chin, chest tight. "I thought you, of all people, would understand my need to pursue my passion. My need to *be* something."

"I did understand it. You had a fledgling online business. I helped you nurture it. What wasn't going to work was to play start-up with a boutique that would take up the lion's share of your time. Our life was too busy."

"*Your* life was. It was never about *my* life. Yours was more important."

"That's not true."

"It damn well is." Champagne sloshed the sides

of her glass as she jabbed it in his direction. "All you wanted was for me to stay in line, to look the part...to warm your bed. And even then, I was a possession to be enjoyed and discarded according to your whims."

His jaw hardened. "Our intimate relationship was the one thing about us that didn't need fixing, *cara mia*. Don't sully it with your sharp tongue."

"Didn't it?" Her mouth twisted. "You never truly let me in—not in bed or out of it. Emotional intimacy was simply not on the table with you."

A glimmer of something she couldn't read passed through those dark eyes. "You are right," he agreed in a clipped tone, "that I, too, bear responsibility for the breakdown of our marriage. We *both* bear responsibility for it. Which is why we're going to fix it together."

Her jaw dropped. "Wh-what?"

"Franco cannot produce an heir. That responsibility falls to me now. Since we are still married, it leaves me with only one option."

Oh, no. She backed away from him. "That's insane. *You* are insane. I'm sorry for Franco, but I am engaged to be married."

"I've just explained why that's impossible."

She absorbed the hard set of his jaw. *My God, he's serious.*

"Lorenzo." She adopted her most reasonable tone. "It can't work between us. We've been through too much. We want different things. I have a life I've built, a career. I'm not giving that up."

"I'm not asking you to give up your career. We'll find some middle ground on that. But I do intend to have my wife back, that part is non-negotiable."

She bit down hard on the inside of her cheek, the salty tang of blood staining her mouth. Once, she would have given anything to hear him say that—that he wanted to fix what they'd broken. In those first few weeks after she'd left, terrified she'd made an irreversible mistake, it had been *all* she'd wanted to hear. But she knew from experience people didn't change. You couldn't heal them no matter how much you loved them. People broke your heart over and over again.

"I won't do it," she said quietly. "You can drag the divorce proceedings out as long as you like, but you're crazy if you think you can just snap your fingers and I'll come back to you and deliver you an heir. I'm engaged, Lorenzo. I'm in love with my fiancé."

Lorenzo absorbed his beautiful wife's lie with the confidence of a man who'd had enough practice reading her reactions to know it was exactly that. A woman didn't pronounce her love for another man and mean it while she ate you up with her eyes like she'd been doing with him. When he could tell he had every nerve in her curvaceous body on edge.

The thought of her offering *that* body to another man made his blood burn. *Watching* her make that toast to her fiancé when she was technically still his. When she would *always* be his.

He dropped his gaze to the thrust of her breasts beneath the delicate silk of her dress. Down over the swell of her hips…the length of her amazing legs atop stiletto heels. His body throbbed with a need that had eluded him for so long his skin went tight at the intensity of it. The injustice of it. *Always Angelina. Never anyone else.*

He returned his gaze to his wife's face, studied the heat that stained her cheeks with a savage satisfaction. "You think," he drawled, "that if

I touched you, I couldn't make you forget about him in about sixty seconds? Because you know I could. There's this thing that happens between us, Angelina, that is undeniable. Pure biological chemistry."

Her mouth tightened, a layer of ice settling over her face. "I'm not playing any more of these games. Byron will be looking for me. I'd advise you to go ahead and have your lawyers fix their mistake or I will sue you and your law firm for incompetence."

A smile twisted his lips. "The thought crossed my mind, too. Then I realized it must be a sign we are meant to fulfill the responsibilities we assumed three years ago."

"You *are* crazy." She spun and walked toward the door. "Get out, Lorenzo, before anyone sees you."

The antagonism in him darkened. She had walked out on him at one of the lowest moments of his life, left him to face a firestorm of Manhattan gossip, to break the news to their family and friends while she'd gone vacationing in the Caribbean. Left their marriage in ashes...

She would not walk out on him again.

"Oh, but I'm not finished." His quiet words stopped her in her tracks. "You didn't think I came here empty-handed did you? Without some bargaining power?"

His wife turned to face him, blue eyes apprehensive. "The Carmichael Company is bleeding money," he told her. "Has been for quite some time. I've given your father two large loans to keep things afloat."

She blinked. "That's impossible."

That had been his reaction when Angie's father had come to him for help. That the Carmichael Company, an over two-hundred-year-old textile dynasty, an American icon with its name on the main campus of one of New York's most prestigious design schools, could be in the red, *deeply* in the red, had been inconceivable to him.

He watched the color drain from his wife's face. "If you bothered to go home, you would know. So many countries are in the mix now, producing high-tech fabrics. Things haven't been good in some time."

She shook her head. "If this is true," she said faintly, "why would you help my family?"

His lips curled. "Because I am loyal to the relationships I form, unlike you. I don't run when things get rocky. Who do you think is underwriting your studio?"

She frowned. "*I* pay the rent on my studio."

"You pay one quarter of the rent. It's my building, Angie."

Her mouth slackened. "I hired that real estate agent. Found the space…"

"You found what I wanted you to." He waved a hand at her. "It made me sleep better at night knowing you were in a safe part of town."

Her face crumpled as realization set in. "What are you insinuating? That you will pull the plug on the aid you're giving to my family, toss me out on the street if I don't agree to come back to you?"

"I prefer to think of it as *incentive*. We owe our marriage a fair shot before we relegate it to the history books. You come back to me, we try and make it work, I pull Carmichael out of its financial difficulties before it becomes a footnote in a list of great American dynasties. It's a win-win."

A win-win? She stared at him, disbelieving. "You would really hold that over my head?"

"You didn't play fair when you walked out on me, *tesoro*. You just cut and ran. So yes, I will use whatever means required to make you see the light. To do the right thing."

"I *asked* you to go to counseling. I *begged* you to. I tried to save our marriage and then I left."

He ignored the stab of guilt that piece of truth pushed through him. "You expected us to solve things overnight. It doesn't happen that way."

Her fingers curled tight around the delicate stem of her champagne flute. "Putting the two of us back in a marriage where we'll destroy one other is not doing the right thing."

"We are both older and wiser. I think we can make it work."

She shook her head. "That's where you're mistaken. That's where you've played the wrong card, Lorenzo, because I will never become your wife again."

She turned on her heel and left. He let her go, because he knew she'd be back. He'd never gambled on a deal he couldn't win.

CHAPTER TWO

ANGIE RETURNED TO the party, shaken to her core. Palms damp, heart thrumming in her chest, a frozen numbness paralyzing her brain, she made a beeline for Abigail. Mouthing an apology to the well-known philanthropist her sister was speaking to, she extracted Abigail from the conversation and pulled her toward a quiet corner of the room.

Her sister eyed her. "What's wrong? You look like you've seen a ghost."

"Lorenzo is here."

Abigail's eyes widened. "At your *engagement* party?"

"Someone screwed up our divorce papers, Abby. We're still married."

"*Married?*" Her sister's jaw dropped. "What do you mean 'screwed them up'? Who?"

"Lorenzo's legal firm. They forgot to file the papers with the state."

"Is he fixing it?"

She closed her eyes. "He won't."

"What do you mean 'won't'?"

"Franco can't have a baby. Lorenzo needs to produce an heir. He wants me to do my duty and put our marriage back together. Give him a baby."

A gasp escaped her sister. "That's outrageous. You're engaged."

"Am I?" Panic skittered up her spine. "If I'm legally married to Lorenzo, what does that make Byron? My *illegitimate* fiancé?"

Her sister looked dumbfounded. "I don't know... Regardless, we'll sic our lawyers on him. This has to be negligence."

"He's angry," she said quietly. "So angry at me for leaving."

"You did what you had to do. Lorenzo wasn't an innocent victim in all this. You both had a role to play in what happened."

Angie pushed a hand through her hair. Fixed her gaze on her sister. "Is the Carmichael Company in trouble? Is there something you haven't been telling me?"

A guarded look wrote itself across her sister's face. "What does that have to do with this?"

"Lorenzo says he's given Father two loans. That

he will bail Carmichael out of its financial problems if I try and make our marriage work. *Incentive*, he called it."

Abby's eyes turned into hard, bright sapphires. "That bastard."

"Is it true? Did he give father those loans?"

"Yes." Her sister's admission made her stomach plunge. "At first it was the need to switch over equipment to compete with other high-tech manufacturers. But Carmichael never really recovered from the new technologies taking over the market."

Angie's breath left her in a sharp exhale. She'd been hoping against hope it wasn't true.

Abigail's lips firmed. "You aren't doing this. Father's been burying his head in the sand for years. He didn't want to see the writing on the wall. It's his problem to fix, not yours."

"Why didn't you tell me?" She swallowed past the lump swelling her throat. "You promised you wouldn't carry the load alone."

"You needed time. You were shattered when you walked away from Lorenzo. The last thing you needed to know was that your ex-husband was bankrolling the Carmichael Company."

Blood pulsed against her temple. "And Mother? How is she handling this?"

Abby frowned. "Ange—"

"Tell me."

"She's become more unstable since the financial difficulties began. It—" She waved a hand. "It may be time to check her into a program. She doesn't want it. She swears she won't go, but I got a call from Sandra last week while they were on a girls' night out. I had to pour her into bed."

Emotions she'd long held at bay welled up inside of her, causing her throat to constrict and the knots in her stomach to twist tighter. "What was it this time?"

"Gin."

She closed her eyes. She'd distanced herself from her family for her own self-preservation—because picking up her mother again and again had left her in a million pieces. Because she just couldn't do it anymore while she'd been trying to pull herself back together after the demise of her marriage. But the guilt surrounding the difficult decisions she'd made was always there in the background, impossible to escape.

It wrapped itself around her now—tight, suffocating. For when Della Carmichael started sliding down her slippery, alcoholic slope, the bottom came fast and furious.

"Angie." Her sister's firm voice brought her head up. "I won't allow him to do this to you. This is not on you."

But Angie knew her sister was wrong. The only solution to this was *her*. Her convincing Lorenzo this was insane, that it would never work. Because she knew tonight hadn't been the end of it.

Her dilemma was still raging in her head as she put down the phone the following evening having assured Byron she was fine—that the headache she'd pleaded to extract herself from the party just before midnight was gone. The same headache that had made her slide out of her fiancé's kiss and leave him on her doorstep, a frown on his face.

Dammit. She gave up on the idea of work, pushed to her feet and walked across her bright studio space to stand looking out at the street. SoHo at night was still busy with foot traffic, the city thick with tourists at the height of the summer. A good thing for the boutique she ran below the studio that featured her work. The bell announcing visitors had been ringing all day.

The purple awning bearing her name whipped in the breeze below. *Carmichael Creations*. It rankled, more than she could say, to know this studio she loved, that she was so proud of, had been contaminated by Lorenzo's powerful reach. She'd wanted—*needed*—to prove so badly she could do this by herself. To follow her heart and forge a successful career as a designer after Lorenzo had dismissed it as a hobby, when in fact, self-expression was as necessary to her as breathing.

She watched a group of young girls walk by, laughing and jabbing each other in the ribs as they pointed at a slick-suited handsome male in front of them. Her heart gave a painful squeeze. She'd been like that when she'd met Lorenzo—desperately innocent, utterly swept away by his powerful aura.

The memories flooded back, tumbling one over another in painful succession until she was standing by the pool at her parents' legendary winter party in Nassau clad in the sexiest silver lamé gown she owned, butterflies in her stomach knowing the gorgeous, ruthless corporate raider

Lorenzo Ricci would be in attendance. Her father had been doing friendly business with Lorenzo rather than serving as one of her husband's hostile takeover targets, but Alistair Carmichael's directive had been clear to his daughter—*leave Lorenzo alone, you're way out of your depth.*

And she had been. But smarting from an argument with her father, needing to escape her miserable, lonely existence for just one night, she couldn't resist. Every woman had wanted to catch Lorenzo, the most desirable widower in Manhattan, perhaps because none ever had. She'd taken her best friend Becka's dare to ask him to dance and shockingly he'd said yes. That dance had led to a kiss in the garden and a hot, heated assignation that had shaken her innocent foundations to the core. She'd gotten her one night with Lorenzo Ricci plus way more than she'd ever bargained for.

She closed her eyes, an ache pulsing low in her chest. She'd thought she could be *the one*, the one who could make her husband love again because what they'd had had seemed earthshaking to her twenty-two-year-old self. That by offering him her unrequited love, she could help him get over his late wife, Lucia, who popular consensus had said he was still hung up on. Until Angelina had learned love was an emotion her husband reserved exclusively for his late wife, an emotion that would never be on offer to her.

Blood throbbed at her temples. She couldn't change the past as much as she wished she could, but she *could*—would—fight Lorenzo on this.

She could postpone the wedding until her divorce came through. Move to a cheaper studio space. But that still didn't address the financial difficulties the Carmichael Company was in. The responsibility that lay on her shoulders.

A chill crawled through her at the thought of the cold, hard stranger she'd faced on the terrace last night. Lorenzo had always been tough, carved by his experiences, shaped by the cutthroat scion of the Ricci family, Salvatore Ricci, but last night she'd seen a whole new lethal side of him.

Had her walking out on Lorenzo made him this heartless? Or was that just the man he'd become?

Guilt fought a battle with anger. Anger won. She'd been right last night—too much had passed between her and Lorenzo to ever resurrect their marriage. He needed to see reason.

She stalked to her desk, pulled her purse out of

the bottom drawer and headed for the door. She was not letting Lorenzo bully her, steal her happiness. Force her back into a life that had nearly destroyed her because he needed an heir for the illustrious Ricci dynasty. She had grown too strong over the past couple of years to let him ride roughshod over her.

Her husband was about to find out just how much she'd changed.

Lorenzo was easy to find. Another hot, steamy Manhattan night bathed the city in a smoky heat as Angie stepped through the doors of her husband's Park Avenue building. The doorman's face lit up when he saw her. Federico's gray brows rose just a fraction before he lowered them back into place and ushered her into the private elevator.

Lorenzo didn't bat an eyelash when the doors opened on the top-floor penthouse. He waved her in as he talked on his headset. As if he'd been expecting her.

Dressed in black jeans and a T-shirt, he looked less corporate shark tonight and more deadly male, the jeans riding low, hugging his lean hips and muscular thighs, his black T-shirt skimming rock-hard abs he kept in premium condition at the gym where he pushed himself as hard as he did everywhere else.

Hell. She banished the frisson of sexual awareness that pulsed through her and walked past him into the luxurious dark brown and chrome space. Lorenzo in casual clothes, which made him look like a mere mortal rather than the deity Wall Street painted him as, had always been her weakness. Perpetuated her belief he had a heart when in fact he did not.

Eyeing the bottle of wine and two glasses that sat on the marble bar, she wondered if he'd been that confident she would show up or whether he'd been expecting someone else. Her stomach contracted into a tight ball. Bringing her back teeth together, she walked to the bar and looked for a bottle of sparkling water in the fridge. Lorenzo covered the microphone and told her to open the wine.

She did. If only to give herself something to do other than absorb the pure physicality of the man pacing the room. She poured two glasses of wine, picked up one and took a sip. Lorenzo rattled off a series of instructions for whoever was on the call and ended it.

"Scusami," he murmured, as he pulled off the headset, tossed it on a chair and walked toward her. "I'm in the middle of negotiations for a company we're looking to acquire."

When wasn't he? "You didn't know I was coming," she said, holding out a glass of the expensive French red he'd provided to put a physical barrier between them. He noted it with an amused twist of his lips.

"I apologize if you were expecting company."

"I was expecting you." Instead of taking the glass, he wrapped his elegant, long-fingered hand around hers and drew her to him.

Her heart slammed against her chest. "Lorenzo…"

He dipped his head toward hers, a dark glimmer of intent in his beautiful eyes. "We forgot our manners last night. Perhaps we should start again."

Her breath caught in her throat. He was going to kiss her. She opened her mouth to protest, to say *absolutely not*, but his firm, sensual lips landed on her cheek instead. Lingered just a little too long for civility's sake...

An electric current charged through her as he repeated the gesture on her other cheek, little pinpricks of heat exploding across her skin. Thoroughly flustered, she stepped back. "I'm not here to accept your proposition."

He lifted a brow. "So you are here to..."

"Talk reason with you."

"All right," he said calmly in the placating tone he'd always used to soothe her like some high-spirited racehorse he'd paid millions for. "Over the wine, then. I've had a hellish day."

Was she allowed to find that secretly enjoyable? She handed him the glass and followed him to the sitting area, where she sank down into one of the chocolate-brown leather chairs she'd always loved to read in.

"What company are you acquiring?"

"The Belmont Hotel Group." He lowered himself into the sofa across from her, splaying his long legs in front of him.

The Belmont? One of the world's most historic luxury hotel chains, it boasted boutique properties in some of the world's most glamorous, exotic locations.

"I'm shocked it's for sale."

"It's not."

"Ah." She took a sip of her wine. "A hostile takeover, then."

"More like a reluctant bride that needs to be brought to heel. She wants to be there but she can't bring herself to admit it."

She eyed him coolly. "Isn't it all the same? It's your specialty, after all. Find a vulnerable company, strip it of its assets, then relegate the rest to the scrap heap. Symbolism, tradition, be damned."

He cocked a brow. "Is this you setting the tone, *cara mia*? I thought you wanted to keep things civil."

She lifted a shoulder. "I don't care for what you do."

"You didn't always feel that way. You used to think it was hot, the power I wield. It was an *aphrodisiac* for you."

Heat stained her cheeks. "And then I grew up. I saw the hundreds of people you put out of jobs. How you relegated iconic companies to the history books if you could profit from it. It was always about the almighty dollar."

"Most of the companies I acquire would eventually fail. It's only a matter of time. In Belmont's case, they have lost sight of what the luxury traveler is looking for—their profits have nose-dived. Call it being cruel to be kind."

"A wolf in sheep's clothing is still a wolf..." She pointed her glass at him. "The question is, when is it all going to be enough, this obsession you have with owning the world?"

He rested his glass on his thigh. "What would you have me do? Rest on my laurels? Tell my shareholders I've proven myself—'so sorry, but that's all the profit you can expect this year...'"

She set her gaze on his. "You could try addressing the demons that drive you."

His dark, spiky lashes swept down. "We aren't here to talk about the past. We're here to discuss our current situation."

"Oh, that's right," she murmured, "that subject is off-limits. I forgot the rules of the game."

His jaw tightened. "Stop baiting me, Angelina, and tell me what's going on in that head of yours."

"Your proposition is outrageous. To expect me

to dissolve my engagement and come back to you, simply to ensure the continuation of the Ricci line..."

He shook his head. "I told you, it's about more than that. It's about both of us putting the effort into this marriage we should have in the first place. About living up to the vows we made."

"You *divorced* me."

"It was a mistake."

Her heart skipped a beat. "What do you mean 'a mistake'?"

"I mean you like to run from your problems, *cara*. And maybe I was running, too. But given the current circumstances, given we are still married, technicality or not, we need to rectify that mistake. I did not intend on marrying twice. I certainly don't intend on marrying a third time."

She came back to reality with a crashing thud. "You don't want me," she said flatly, "you know that. You want a nice little Italian wife your mother will love who will host your dinner parties, charm your business acquaintances and greet you at the door every night in sexy lingerie. *That* would be your idea of perfection."

An amused glint entered his gaze. "I'm fairly

sure I would be bored with an obedient wife after you. But you are right on the lingerie—that *would* be my idea of perfection."

She said a very bad word in her head. "You don't even know who I am anymore. I'm different. Changed. Not the woman you married, nor will I ever be again."

"Then I look forward to finding out who that woman is." He gave her an appraising look. "I'm prepared to make concessions to make this work. Your career is a case in point. You've clearly become very successful. You've worked hard to get where you are. As long as it doesn't interfere with our important commitments, we'll make it work."

We'll make it work? Heat rose up inside of her. He had no idea what her work meant to her. The sanity it had been throughout her rocky life.

"As for my mother," he continued, "she had certain...*preconceived* notions regarding our marriage you never dispelled with your behavior. You also never made an effort with her. If you do so, I expect you'll find her a different woman."

Her fingers curled into a fist. "She thought I deliberately trapped you into marriage."

"Not an unreasonable assumption when our one

night together resulted in a pregnancy. I did, however, make it clear that the responsibility lay on both of us."

"How big of you." A red mist of fury wrapped itself around her brain. "What other *concessions* are you prepared to make, Lorenzo? Are you prepared to let me beneath that impenetrable layer of yours? Talk to me instead of shutting me out? Confront our issues instead of pushing me to the outer fringes of your life until I cease to exist?"

"Yes." The low rumble in his voice vibrated through her. "I understand I was distant at times... emotionally unavailable if you like. I recognize that as a fault of mine I need to work on. But let's just be clear, Angelina, you locked me out just as surely as I ever did you with those cast-iron defenses of yours."

After the big chill had begun. Because eventually it had become too painful to give and never get anything back.

Hurt contracted the muscles around her heart. The wine warming her blood, loosening her inhibitions, made her reckless. "If we're going for the brutal truth here," she growled, "if we're not going to pull our punches, then let's get all the skeletons out on the table shall we? The real reason our marriage failed was Lucia. Because you would have preferred to stay in your cave, pining for your dead wife. Instead you had to marry me."

The color leached from his olive skin. His face tightened, cheekbones standing out like blades. The cold fire that engulfed his dark eyes told her she'd gone too far this time. "It was *your* obsession with Lucia that you wouldn't let go of, not mine."

Her chin lifted, heart pounding in her chest. "Tell yourself that enough and you might even start to believe it."

The silence in the room was deafening. Chest tight, she pushed to her feet and crossed to the floor-to-ceiling windows that framed a magnificent view of Central Park lit up at night. Hugging her arms around herself, she took a deep breath and attempted to regain her equilibrium.

"You aren't this heartless," she said after a long moment, turning to face him. "I don't believe you will let the Carmichael Company fail. You like my father too much."

His eyes were a purposeful, dark velvet cool. "Then don't make me. I meant what I said, Angie.

I want you back. I want us to give this marriage the shot it deserves. You come back to me with your heart and head fully in it and I will ensure your legacy survives."

The confusion swirling in her head deepened, thickened. She wrapped her arms tighter around herself, struggled to contain her emotions, but they spilled outside of the edges of her barely shored-up walls. "Wasn't it enough for you?" she asked, voice trembling. "Every second, every minute of those last excruciating months together? We couldn't even be in the same room without tearing each other's throats out. And when we did, it didn't feel any better...it felt worse."

He got to his feet and prowled toward her. "We lost a baby. It was painful, Angelina, it *hurt*."

A rock climbed into her throat. "And here we are hurting each other again."

He stopped centimeters from her. Her body reacted to the heat of him, the familiarity of him, vibrating with an internal memory she couldn't control. She pressed her fingers to her cheeks, trying to hold it in, trying to stop the insanity midflow, but he saw it, read her as he always had, eyes darkening with heat.

"The point is to get past the pain. To deal with what we should have dealt with years ago."

"No," she said, shaking her head, fear bubbling up inside of her like magma, threatening to push her on a course she knew she'd regret. "I'm engaged, Lorenzo. I love him."

Fire licked his gaze. "You know that's a lie."

"It's not a lie. It's the truth."

"You are my *wife*." Curving an arm around her waist, he drew her to him. She swallowed as her vibrating body swayed perilously close to the wall of heat that drew her like a moth to a flame. She flattened a palm against his chest, but her feet wouldn't seem to take her anywhere and her eyes locked on his. "Kiss me like you don't belong to me," he said huskily, "and I might reconsider."

"No." Her sharp response sounded as panicked as she felt. "Why are you doing this? Why are you being so cruel?"

"Because I should have stopped you the first time you walked out. Because the thought of you with another man drives me insane…because you *haunt* me, Angelina, every time I'm with another woman. All I can see is those beautiful blue eyes of yours and those vows we recited…" He cupped her jaw in his hand, fingers closing possessively over her skin. "Because we are not over, *mi amore*. We never will be."

Her heart stuttered, an ache enveloping her that seemed to go soul-deep. "You can't do this to me," she said hoarsely. "Throw threats at me one minute, then say these things the next and just expect me to—"

He lowered his head, breath mingling with hers. "Prove you feel nothing for me. Prove what I'm saying isn't true and I'll walk away."

"No." But even as she said it, his mouth was covering hers in a whisper-soft caress that switched on every cell in her body. She closed her eyes. *Just do it, Angie. Prove it to him, then walk away.*

He slid a hand up her back, flattened his big palm against her spine. Warm, possessive, his touch seeped into her senses, stroked a wounded, jagged part of her that had never healed. Warning bells went off in her head, a blaring, unmistakable cautionary signal she should stop this now. But she had to convince him it was over.

Slow, infinitely gentle nudges of his mouth demanded a response. She held herself rigid, determined to end it. Tightening his fingers around her jaw, he tilted her head back and took a deeper possession of her mouth. The alarm bells in her head grew louder as the sweet intoxication of his kiss melted her bones.

"Lorenzo—"

He slicked his tongue across her lower lip. Erotic, intimate, it sent shock waves of pleasure rocketing through her. Her mind blanked, stomach clenched, fingers curling around a handful of his T-shirt. He did it again, stroking soft, vulnerable flesh with a deliberate possession that made her quiver.

When he flicked his tongue along the seam of her lips and demanded entry, she obeyed, lost in a sea of sensation. He rewarded her with a hot, toe-curling caress that made her moan low in her throat, grab hold of him more firmly.

He brought her closer with the palm of his hand at her back. Swept it down to cup the flesh of her buttock. The kiss turned needy, desperate, her hips arching against his burgeoning arousal. Thick, hard, he was so potently virile he turned her blood to fire.

Reality slammed into her like a bucket of ice dropped over her head. She shoved a hand against his chest and pushed back. Breathless, her mouth bruised from his kisses, she stood staring at him.

How had that happened? How had she *let* that happen?

"I hate you," she breathed. "I really do."

His mouth twisted. "That makes two of us. Sometimes I really hate you, too, *tesoro*. It's the rest of the time that messes us up."

She shook her head. Backed away from him. Turning, she snatched her purse off the chair and walked out without looking back.

What had she done?

CHAPTER THREE

New York Daily Buzz
Society Shocker!

Word has it the engagement of up-and-coming designer Angelina Carmichael and district attorney candidate Byron Davidson is off after a flashy soiree to celebrate the couple's betrothal just two weeks ago.

The buzz about town is the prominent lawyer is clearly devastated at the split, perhaps suggesting it was Angelina who called it off?

One can't help but wonder if the reason for the break comes in the form of none other than Angelina's ex: sexy corporate raider Lorenzo Ricci. The two were seen dining at Tempesta Di Fuoco last week, conjuring up images of the couple's tempestuous marriage that offered this column a regular supply of juicy news over its fiery but short duration.

Given the much lusted-after Lorenzo has been curiously devoid of a woman on his arm since the split, suspicion is running rampant that Angelina could be the cause.

The question on everyone's lips is...are the Riccis back on?

OH, FOR GOODNESS' SAKE. Angie tossed the salacious tabloid on the coffee table in her studio, blood heating. Did those people not have better things to do with their time? Her heart sank as she imagined what Byron must be thinking. *Feeling.* How he was coping with the barrage of gossip that had spread through town faster than a forest fire eating up dry timber.

She hadn't talked to him since the night after her confrontation with Lorenzo, when she'd given him back his ring. Since that *kiss* with her husband had made it clear she couldn't marry her fiancé. Even if Lorenzo had miraculously changed his mind and offered to expedite their divorce, she still couldn't have married her fiancé. Not after everything she'd done to prove she was over her husband, that she didn't care about him anymore, had been exposed for the lie it was.

Her mouth turned down. *That* was why she'd

felt so off the night of the engagement party. Because she'd been trying to convince herself she was in love with her ultraintelligent, grounded fiancé, that she wanted the opposite of her rollercoaster ride of a marriage, when in fact she had never truly gotten over Lorenzo—the man who had made her feel as if her emotions were out of control.

The movers, currently emptying her apartment above the studio of her possessions, stomped back in to take the final load of boxes out to the truck parked on the street. The ball of tension in her stomach grew as she witnessed what was left of her carefully constructed existence disappear before her eyes.

A conversation with her father had provided no alternatives to her husband's proposition, only a suggestion by her father to repair the marriage she never should have left in the first place.

Potential investors were too spooked by Carmichael Company's recent performance to touch the once lauded company, nor would her father's pride allow him to hunt other offers of assistance. Which meant, as she'd feared, she was the only solution to this problem if her brother, James, who would someday soon run Carmichael Company and her sister, Abigail, were to have anything left of the company to inherit.

She picked up her coffee, taking a sip of the steaming brew and cradling the cup in her hands. Allowing Abigail to bear all the responsibility for her mother was also something she needed to fix. She had her life together now. She was strong. It was time to start assuming some of the responsibilities she'd been shirking so her sister could have a life, too.

Which didn't negate the fear gripping her insides. The anger keeping her awake at night, tossing in her bed, leaving her hollow-eyed in the morning. That Lorenzo was forcing her into this reconciliation, using her family as leverage, made his intentions very clear. This was a power play for him like every other he executed on a daily basis. He wanted her back, needed his heir, so he'd made it happen.

It was not about his feelings for her. Or lack of them... About a sentimental, real desire to give what they'd had a second chance. It was about him repossessing what he felt was his. Staking his claim.

She set down her cup in its saucer. If she was going to do this, she needed to do it with her eyes wide-open, naïveté firmly banished. On *her* terms. She wasn't going to allow him to take control, to overwhelm and intimidate her as he had the first time around. She wasn't sacrificing the independence and freedom she'd carved out for herself and she wasn't letting her husband break her heart again. Those were her *rules.*

Defiance drove her back to her worktable when the movers left, where her anger fueled a furious burst of productivity. By the time she finished up a couple of pieces for Alexander Faggini's Fashion Week show, her watch read 7:00 p.m. *Oops.* She was supposed to be home having dinner with Lorenzo right now—their first night together again in the penthouse. Unfortunately, she was going to be at least a half hour late.

"How's the deal going? Still mired in legalese?"

"*Sì.*" Lorenzo cradled his mobile between ear and shoulder while he poured himself a drink in deference to the end of the week. "There's a few small points Bavaro and I have to work through. He's been a bit of a wild card."

"Bene." Amusement danced in Franco's voice. "I love watching Father on this one. To make Ricci the largest luxury hotel chain in the world is an accomplishment even he can't match. It kills him to think of you surpassing his achievements."

Lorenzo smiled. His father, retired now and serving on the boards of other companies, had an endless thirst for competition. That included the one he had with his sons. It had made the bonds between him and Franco even tighter as they had united to combat their father's powerful personality, with Franco running the shipping operations out of Milan, while Lorenzo oversaw the rest of the company from New York.

"He needn't worry he'll be forgotten. He has more than his fair share of achievements." Lorenzo lifted the whiskey to his mouth and took a sip. "So," he said, as the fiery spirit burned a soothing path through his insides, "when were you going to tell me about the IVF? I have to hear it from the old man?"

A low oath. "I should have known he'd jump the gun. We didn't get the results on the latest procedure until today. I was waiting until we knew for sure before laying that on you."

"I figured it was something like that." He paused a beat, searching for the right words. "So what was the verdict?"

"It didn't work. Likely never will."

A knot formed in his throat. "*Mi dispiace.* I know how much you and Elena wanted this."

"It is what it is."

The raspy edge to his brother's voice gutted him. It always hurt to be so far away but right now it felt like the sharp blade of a knife. "How is Elena taking the news?"

"Not well. She's claiming it's her fault even though I've told her it could just as easily be me."

He closed his eyes. He didn't know the pain of being denied what he'd always assumed to be his, but he did know what it was like to lose a baby. How deeply it had cut when just a week after being given a clean bill of health, Angelina had inexplicably lost their child. How you didn't know how much you wanted something until it was taken away from you.

"Be there for her," he said quietly. Do what he hadn't done.

Franco exhaled. "We might adopt. I don't know… it's a big step."

"It is. Take your time with it."

A pause. Franco's tone was wary when he spoke. "Your reconciliation with Angelina… The timing is…"

"It's not because of this. Yes, there is that, but it's become clear to me Angelina and I have unfinished business between us."

"She walked out on you, *fratello*. How much more finished do you want it to be?"

Lorenzo winced, pressed a hand to his temple. "I bear responsibility for the demise of my marriage, too. You know I have my ghosts."

"*Sì.* But she changed you, Lorenzo. You shut down after she left. You don't trust like you used to—you aren't the same man."

No, he wasn't. His wife had taken a piece of him with her when she'd walked out that door on the heels of the loss of his child, his fledgling trust in life and love, his half-built bond with Angelina vaporizing on a tide of bitterness so thick he'd wondered if he would ever move past it. But with time, as his grief over Lucia had subsided, his own faults had been revealed. It would be delusional of him to lay the blame solely at his wife's feet.

"Angie was young. She needed time to grow. I intend for our marriage to work this time."

"Or you will take the house down around you as you try." A wry note stained his brother's voice.

Lorenzo asked about his mother's upcoming birthday celebrations. They chatted about that for a few minutes before his brother signed off. Lorenzo leaned against the bar and nursed his drink while he waited for his wife to deign to appear.

The thought that he would have to produce the Ricci heir no longer evoked the violent reaction it had when his father had lobbed that grenade at him. Instead of feeling *roped and tied*, he felt strangely satisfied. As if his father's directive had been the incentive he had needed to rewrite a piece of history that hadn't gone down as it should have.

Two years after the death of Lucia, he had still been without a taste for women the night he'd met Angelina in Nassau. Plagued by demons, if the truth be known, over the wife he hadn't protected. Until Angie had walked out on the terrace while he'd been talking to one of her father's associates and he'd felt as if he'd been struck by lightning.

All it had taken was one dance, his hands taking purchase of her lush curves, before he'd found himself in an isolated part of the gardens taking over the seduction, driven by a need he couldn't name. His libido had woken up like a five-alarm blaze by the time they'd made it to his luxurious room on the Carmichael estate. Somehow, in the haze of his still ever-present grief, Angie had brought him back to life.

His mouth twisted as he brought the whiskey to his lips. Little had he known that the passion they shared would devolve into the plot from *The War of the Roses*. That the only place he and his young wife would be in sync was in the bedroom, where they'd solved every argument with hot, burn-your-clothes-off sex.

The clock chimed seven thirty. His good mood began to evaporate. The elevator doors swished open a couple of minutes later, his wife breezing in dressed in black capris and a sparkly, peasant-style blouse. Her hair pulled back in a ponytail, face devoid of makeup, she was still the most exquisite woman he'd ever known.

"Long day?" he drawled, leashing his anger.

Pink color stained her cheeks. "It was. I had

to finish up some pieces for a show. I'm sorry I'm late."

No, she wasn't. But for the sake of their fresh start and given everything he'd thrown at her, he cut her some slack. "Go change." He cocked his head toward the bedroom. "Constanza unpacked your things. She left dinner in the oven. It'll keep while we have a drink."

Her eyes darkened at the order. Firming her mouth, she dropped her purse on a chair and swept by him.

"Angie?"

She swung around.

"Put your wedding rings on."

She lifted her chin. "Is this how it's going to be, Lorenzo? Just like old times? You firing orders at me? Expecting me to run and do your bidding?"

"Married people wear wedding rings." He held up his left hand, the elegant, simple gold band she had given him glittering in the light.

Her face tightened. Turning on her heel, she disappeared down the hallway. When she returned, she was dressed in the comfortable black leggings she favored and a cream-colored tunic that fell just below her curvaceous derriere. *Un-*

fortunate, he decided. He'd have to fill in that part from memory.

"Drink?" he asked, walking to the bar.

"Mineral water, please."

"It's Friday night."

"I'd still like mineral water."

And the battle lines were drawn… He poured it for her, added a slice of lime and carried it out onto the terrace, where Angie had drifted. Strategically placed lanterns lit up a thirty-five-million-dollar view of the park.

He handed her the drink. Noted she wore her sapphire engagement ring and wedding band. "Which show?"

She blinked. "Sorry?"

"Which show are you designing for?"

"Oh." She wrapped her fingers around the glass. "Alexander Faggini's Fashion Week show."

"That's impressive."

She lifted a shoulder. "A friend of mine introduced us. He thought my designs worked well with his. It's an honor for me."

"I'd like to see the collection."

"Would you?" She turned those beautiful blue

eyes on him. "Or are you just making an effort to appear interested?"

"Angelina," he growled.

"It's a fair question." Her chin set at a belligerent angle. "I am, after all, *playing at a start-up* business that has somehow, magically, found success."

He rested his gaze on hers. "Three-quarters of new businesses fail in this city. They don't even last until their second year. You have done something extraordinary with yours. I'm proud of you. But at the time, it seemed like a long shot."

"You didn't think I had the talent? Not even with you *nurturing* me?"

There was a distinctly wounded edge to her eyes now. He blew out a breath. "I could see you were talented. But you knew I wanted my wife at home. We were having a baby."

"You were like that after we lost the baby. When I desperately needed something to occupy my brain."

His mouth flattened. "I could have supported you better, there's no question about it. I *should* have. But someone had to run our life. I needed the sanity of you at home."

"And I needed the sanity my work provided

me." She turned her gaze to the lush canvas of green spread out before them, Central Park in full, glorious bloom.

He studied the delicate line of her jaw, the stubborn set of her mouth, silhouetted in the lamplight. *Defensive. Protective.* It made him wonder about all the pieces of his wife he hadn't known. Didn't know. Had never attempted to know.

"Sanity from what?"

She shrugged. "My life. All of it."

He frowned. He understood what being the offspring of a dynasty meant, because his family was as much Italian aristocracy as the Carmichaels were American royalty. Understood how the pressure of the relentless press coverage, the high expectations, the *rules* in their world could weigh a person down. What he had never understood was what about it his wife reacted so violently to.

"Why do you hate it so much," he asked, sweeping a hand through the air. "This world? Why has being a Carmichael been so difficult for you? I could never figure it out. I know you have a combative relationship with your father and that having his affairs plastered across the media couldn't be easy for you…but it always seemed like it was more."

A cynical light shone in her gaze as she turned toward him. "Did it need to be more? Those affairs devastated my mother, cut her so deeply she never recovered."

"No," he agreed, "it doesn't. My father worships the ground my mother walks on and rightly so. I can't imagine how painful it must have been to watch your father disrespect your mother like that when she has stood by his side the entire time."

Her dark lashes swept over her cheeks. "You see what everyone else sees. The glittering, perfect world of the Carmichaels. You don't see the dysfunction on the inside."

"So tell me about it," he countered. "Help me understand."

"They are private family issues. I would be betraying confidences if I did."

"You are my *wife*. You can confide in me."

Her mouth formed a stubborn, straight line. An oath left his lips. "This is one of those areas we need to fix, Angelina. How can we make this marriage work if there are big pieces of you I don't know?"

"Like those big pieces of you I don't know?" Her eyes flashed, a storm rising in their gray-blue depths. "You can't press a button and summon emotional intimacy. *Trust.* It doesn't work like that. It takes time and effort. If you want that from me, you have to lead by example."

Heat seared his belly. He knew she was right. Knew he'd been operating on automatic pilot in the years after Lucia's death, cauterizing his emotions, refusing to feel. But it wasn't the easiest thing to admit.

"Bene," he conceded harshly, opening his arms wide. "Consider me an open book, then. No subject is off-limits. Anything is fair game. But we *are* going to learn how to communicate—in ways that do not involve the bedroom."

The stare she leveled at him rattled every nerve ending. Made him ache to resort to tried-and-true methods. But he wasn't going there. He was making good on the promise he'd just given her.

"I think," he said evenly, deciding a change of subject was in order, "we should host a party in the Hamptons over the long weekend. Marc Bavaro, the CEO of the Belmont chain, has a place there. I'd like to try and soften him up a bit. Get a few outstanding issues resolved. It would also provide an ideal opportunity to formally announce our reconciliation given the gossip that's running rampant."

She muttered something under her breath. His brow lifted. *"Scusa?"*

"I *said* to put your stamp on me. That's why you want to have this party."

"I already did that," he murmured, eyes on hers. "Why would I need to make a public display of ownership when we both know the truth?"

A flush stained her cheeks. "Go to hell, Lorenzo."

"I've already been there, *cara*. At least this time there will be a great deal of pleasure along with the pain."

Her eyes locked with his. A long, loaded moment passed as they took a step into uncharted territory. Lashes lowered, his wife studied him, as if deciding whether to continue the charge.

Her chin dropped. "Everyone's calendars will be full on the Labor Day weekend."

"They'll be doing the rounds. What's one more stop? Speculation about us alone will pack them in."

She gave him a pointed look as if to say that was exactly the issue. "I have to finish the pieces for Alexander so he can match them up with the show. If something doesn't work, I'll need to come up with an alternative."

"It's one weekend. There's nothing pressing between now and then. Work around it." He pointed his whiskey glass at her. "This is where we learn to compromise, Angie. You give, I give—that's how it works."

Her mouth flattened. "Fine."

"Good. Gillian will plan it, you will contribute your guest list and the staff in the Hamptons will execute. All you need to do is show up."

Her expression remained frozen. He sought the patience he was not known for. "I expect you to invite your family. Whatever's going on between you and your parents, you need to fix it. This will be a good opportunity to do so."

"No." The word flew out of her mouth—swift and vehement. He lifted a brow. "I went to see them last week," she explained. "They aren't in the Hamptons much anymore in the summer. There's no point in inviting them."

"I'm sure they'll make the effort to come. It will look strange if they're not there given I do business with your father." He took a sip of his whiskey. "Speaking of parents, mine will be visiting the week after the party. They'll stay at their apartment, but we'll host them here for dinner. Decide on a date with Gillian that works for you."

Her face fell further, if that was possible. "What did you tell them? About us?"

"That we've decided to make this marriage work. That we made a decision in haste at a time when we were both in pain and now we are rectifying it."

"So you chose to leave out the part where you're *bullying* me into becoming your wife again?"

"I prefer to think of it as a mutually beneficial arrangement. *Motivation* for us to make this marriage work." He leveled his gaze on her combative face. "We made a deal, a commitment to each other, Angelina. I meant it when I said your heart and soul have to be in it, but I'm not so unfeeling that I don't understand you need time to adjust. After that settling-in period, however, I expect an *attitude* adjustment, because this is not how it's going to be."

* * *

An attitude adjustment? Angie was still fuming after she and Lorenzo had shared a tense, mostly silent dinner on the terrace, where she ate little and talked less. It had been so *generous* of him to concede she needed time and space after what he'd done to her. *Clearly* she should be falling into line, looking forward to spending more time with his PA than she did her husband.

Her mouth twisted. *I meant it when I said your heart and soul have to be in it.* He didn't even *have* a heart…or a soul for that matter. What would he know about it?

Lorenzo was ensconced in his home office to finish some work, so she elected to have a hot bath and go to bed. Constanza had unpacked all her things in the light, airy master bedroom, with its gorgeous vistas of the park, the housekeeper's usual ruthless efficiency putting everything back as if she'd never left.

It was eerie to pull a nightgown from a puddle of silk in a drawer and untangle her hair with the pearl-backed brush that sat on the dresser in the exact same place it used to be. On edge, her nerves in disarray, she headed for a rose-scented bath in the Italian-tiled en suite, immersing herself up to her ears in hot, cathartic bubbles.

All sarcasm aside, she was relieved with her husband's acknowledgment they needed time—that he didn't expect her to jump into bed with him as seamlessly as her brush had landed back on the dresser. But clearly, she thought, stomach knotting, given that her things were where they were, he expected her to share that bed with him. The thought made her search desperately for something else to focus on, like why he had rose-scented bath bubbles in here.

Either Constanza had been thoughtful, as she was wont to be, or they had belonged to one of his lovers. Because surely, the tabloids couldn't be right? Surely her highly sexual husband, who'd thought he was divorced, had had other women?

You haunt me, Angelina, every time I'm with another woman... Her heart sank, a numb feeling settling over her. He'd pretty much admitted he had. Lorenzo wouldn't have spent two years pining after her as she had him. Going dateless until Byron wouldn't take no for an answer.

The thought of her husband with other women lanced her insides. She sank farther into the bubbles and closed her eyes. They had been so happy in the beginning. That's what hurt the most. What *might* have been.

After Lorenzo had accepted the consequences of what a broken condom had produced, he'd submitted willingly to her mother's ostentatious society wedding—what he'd considered a politically advantageous match, she suspected. She'd been too crazy about him to care.

They'd spent the first months of their marriage in a pheromone-induced haze, tuning out the world. In Lorenzo's arms, her worries about why he'd married her had faded to black. He'd hungered after her with an intensity that had made her feel as if she'd been the most important thing on the planet to him, their addictive obsession with each other inescapable, unassailable. The wounded pieces of her, the parts that had been convinced she was unlovable after a childhood devoid of emotion, had begun to heal. For the first time in her life, she'd felt whole, as if she was *worthy* of love.

And how could she not? Having her husband focus on her, choose to engage, had been like having the most powerful force in the universe directed at her. Suddenly all the pieces of her life had been falling into place and happiness had seemed attainable after years of wondering if it even existed.

Until reality had interceded—one of Lorenzo's big, flashy deals had come along, he'd immersed himself in it and their cozy cocoon had become her husband's insanely busy life.

She'd learned being Mrs. Lorenzo Ricci had meant wining and dining his business contacts multiple times a week, their social schedule so exhausting for a pregnant Angie she'd barely been able to keep up. She'd begun to feel as if she was drowning, but Lorenzo hadn't seemed to care, was too busy to notice.

It had all come to a head when they'd lost their baby. Her increasingly distant husband withdrew completely, rendering him a virtual stranger. He'd descended into the blackness, whatever hell had been consuming him, and they'd never recovered. But, apparently, she thought bitterly, it was *her* obsession with Lucia that had crippled their marriage—not his.

The water cooling, a chill descending over her, she got out of the bath and got ready for bed. Slipping the silk nightie over her head, her eyes were half-closed by the time she stood in front of the beautiful, chrome, four-poster bed.

Too many memories crowding her head, a burn in her chest so painful it was hard to breathe, she fought back the hot, fat tears that burned her eyes. *I can't do it.* She could no more get into that bed as if the last two years hadn't happened than she could convince herself that coming back to Lorenzo hadn't been a big, huge mistake.

She padded down the hall to the guest room. Done in soothing pale blues and yellow, it evoked none of the master bedroom's painful echoes. Pulling back the silk coverlet, she slid between the sheets. Peace descended over her. She was out like a light in minutes.

She woke to a feeling of weightlessness. Disoriented, half-asleep, she blinked against the velvet black of night. Registered the strong arms that cradled her against a wall of muscle. *Heat.* The subtle, spicy, familiar scent seduced her into burrowing closer. *Lorenzo.*

Lost in the half-awake state that preceded full consciousness, bereft of time and place, the dark, delicious aroma of her husband seeping into her senses, she flattened her palm against the hard planes of his chest. Reveled in his strength. Registered the rigid set of his body against hers.

Her eyes flew open, consciousness slamming into her swift and hard. The taut line of Lorenzo's jaw jolted her the rest of the way to full alertness. Cold, dark eyes that glittered like diamonds in the dim light.

"Wh-what are you doing?" she stuttered as he carried her down the hallway and into the master bedroom.

He dumped her on the bed. "You can have all the time you need but you will sleep in here. We are moving *forward*, not backward."

She pressed a hand into the mattress and pushed herself upright. "I—" She slicked her tongue over her lips. "I couldn't get into this bed. There were too many memories, too many things I—"

"What?" he responded harshly. "Too many things you want to forget? Too much backstory you'd like to erase instead of facing it?"

She blinked, her eyes becoming accustomed to the light. Anger pulsed in his face—a living, breathing entity that made her heart tick faster. "Why are you so angry?"

"You weren't in bed," he said tersely. "I didn't know where you were."

He'd thought she'd left. Again. The realization wrote itself across her brain in a dazed discovery that had her studying those hot, furious eyes. She'd known instinctively that walking out on Lorenzo hadn't been the right thing to do, but she hadn't been equipped with the emotional maturity at twenty-three to handle the destruction they had wrought. Instead she had left Lorenzo alone to face the fallout of their marriage while she'd spent a month in the Caribbean with her grandmother. She'd never quite forgiven herself for it.

"I'm sorry," she said quietly, reminding herself he had things to be angry about, too. "For leaving like that. I didn't handle it the right way. I did what I thought was necessary at the time. I needed to find myself—to discover who I was. But it wasn't right. I know that."

He reached for the top button of his shirt, eyes on hers. "And did you succeed? Did you find what you were looking for?"

"Yes." She laced her fingers together, eyes dropping to the sapphire that blazed on her finger. "I found me."

"And who is she?"

"The true me," she said quietly. "The one who spends her evenings with a sketch pad beside the bed, who gets to get up every morning and make those ideas into reality, tells a story someone might find beautiful. That's what I love, Lorenzo. That's when I am at peace."

He stared at her for a long moment, then finished unbuttoning his shirt. She told herself to look away as he stripped it off, but her sleepy, hazy brain, her senses, still filled with the scent of him, the parts of her that still craved him like a drug demanded she watch. Absorb every lean, cut line he exposed, angling down to the V that disappeared into his belt line.

Heat lifting to her face, she lay back against the pillows. It didn't matter how many times she'd seen Lorenzo naked, it still had the ability to fluster her beyond reason.

Seeking to distract herself, she voiced the one question her still unguarded brain needed to know as she lay staring at the ceiling. "Those women you talked about...did you sleep with them?"

* * *

Lorenzo balled up his T-shirt and tossed it in the hamper, struggling to get his anger under control. A part of him, the bitter, wounded part that hadn't been able to enjoy the one woman he had taken to bed during their time apart, while she had apparently found her fiancé more than satisfactory, wanted to see her flinch, *hurt*. But something stopped him. He thought it might be the knowledge that if he followed through on that desire, it would haunt them forever.

Setting his knee down on the bed, he joined his wife. "I don't think we should go there," he said softly. "I said, forward, Angie, not back."

Her face crumpled. "I want to know."

A knot formed in his chest. He drew in a breath. *Dannazione*—he was not the injured party here.

"One," he said evenly, "and no, I won't tell you who she is."

"Why?"

"Because you don't need to know."

She closed her eyes.

Heat seared his belly. Blood fizzling in his veins, he threw a thigh over his wife's silk-clad body and caged her in, forearms braced on either side of her head. "Angelina," he murmured, watching as her eyes fluttered open, "you asked. And while we're at it, let's not forget about our friend Byron."

Her lashes shaded her cheeks. "I didn't sleep with Byron. We were waiting."

He rocked back on his heels. "Waiting for *what*?"

"Until we got married."

Incredulity that any man would marry a woman without knowing whether they were sexually compatible warred with the infuriating knowledge that she had lied to him.

"And yet you deliberately let me think you'd bedded him," he murmured. "'I have no complaints,' was how I think you put it."

Her eyes filled with an icy blue heat. "You blackmailed me back into this marriage, Lorenzo. If you think I'm going to apologize, think again."

What he *thought* was that he had no idea what to think. Knowing his wife remained his and only his satisfied him on a level he couldn't even begin to articulate. That she might be as haunted by him as he was by her...

He traced his gaze over her lush, vulnerable

mouth. Across the enticing stretch of bare skin the askew neckline of her nightie revealed, down over the smooth flesh of her thighs where the silk had ridden up...the dusky shadow between her legs. *Unbearable temptation.* Hard as rock, he ached for her.

"Get off me." His wife drew his attention back up to her flushed face.

His lip curled. "What's the matter, *mia cara?* You afraid I'm going to penetrate those defenses you cling so desperately to? That make you feel so *safe?*"

A defiant look back. "Just like yours do?"

"Ah, but *I* am promising to open up." A lazy smile twisted his lips. "I'm a caterpillar poised for transformation. You get to come out of your cocoon, too, and try your wings."

"Very funny." She pushed at his chest. *"Off."*

He dropped his mouth to her ear. "An open book, Angelina. That's what you and I are going to be. The brutal truth and nothing but. We might just survive this little experiment if we can offer each other that."

He levered himself off his sexy, furious wife and headed for the bathroom. It occurred to him, then, as he stepped under a hot shower, his emotions a tangled mess, that he might have underestimated the power his wife still held over him. That both of them might end up getting burned before this was over.

CHAPTER FOUR

ANGIE SPENT THE WEEK leading up to the Hamptons party attempting to avoid any further confrontations between her and Lorenzo. That combustible scene in their bedroom had convinced her engaging with her husband was not a good strategy. Avoidance was. And with Lorenzo immersed in his big deal, it hadn't proven difficult. It was almost like old times.

Except it wasn't. She had been working long hours, too, at the studio getting Alexander's collection ready, with Lorenzo's support. Her husband, however, had insisted they share dinners together, even if they had to work afterward. He was intent, it seemed, on making this marriage work. They talked, shared things about their day, managed, for the most part, to be civil. But soon afterward, Lorenzo retreated to his office to work, not coming to bed until the early hours, ensuring her strategy had worked perfectly.

Tonight, however, she conceded as she watched a perfect East Hampton sunset stain the sky, there would be no escaping—not from her combustive relationship with her husband, nor the past she'd worked so hard to leave behind. Tonight they would host the toast of high society for cocktails at their sprawling waterfront estate, an event that had the gossip hounds frothing at the mouth and her insides curling in an intense, visceral reaction that begged her to retreat.

But it was too late. It had been too late ever since Gillian had sent out the cream-and-silver embossed invitations via courier and the RSVPs had started flooding in by the dozens, proving Lorenzo's point that a helping of titillating gossip would always command the day.

She watched a graceful, forty-foot sailboat navigate past on the gray-blue Shinnecock Bay, the high waves and white foam a perfect mirror for her churning insides. She adored the peace and tranquility of this exclusive enclave, the ability to escape a tourist-infested, muggy Manhattan and enjoy the cool breezes that tempered the island. What she didn't enjoy was the microcosm of Manhattan society the Hamptons were at this time of year. Taking part in the requisite social circuit, forging the right contacts through her and Lorenzo's recreational activities, *being seen with the right crowd.*

"You might as well be at work," her entrepreneurial friend, Cassidy, had once said, referring to the intense networking that went on here 24/7. "At least in Manhattan, you can disappear into your town house, plead a prior engagement and no one will ever know. In the Hamptons, *everyone* knows."

Her mouth twisted. And the cliquishness? The competitiveness? The feckless alliances that changed with the wind? She had seen the devastation they could wreak, had watched her mother shredded by their vicious bite and yet Bella Carmichael had, unfathomably, always gone back for more because headlining an American dynasty wasn't something you just walked away from.

Her mother had learned to grit her teeth and smile as all Carmichaels did, even when her world was falling apart, pretending the gossip chasing through the room about Alistair Carmichael's infidelities, which of his "assistants" he was sleeping with now, didn't faze her in the least. That her husband's predilection for twenty-five-year-old blondes and the power that came along with his ability to command them was par for the course in the world they lived in.

She smoothed clammy palms over her cranberry-red silk dress, praying her father's indiscretions would not come up tonight. She'd already briefed the waitstaff her mother was not to be served alcohol under any circumstance. Watching her go off the rails in front of the upper echelons of Manhattan society was the last thing she needed.

"I like this dress." Lorenzo materialized behind her, his hands settling on her hips. "Although," he drawled, turning her around, his inspection dipping to the plunging neckline of the dress, "I'm not sure I'm going to appreciate every other man in attendance tonight enjoying the same view."

Her pulse fluttered in her throat. Heat radiated from the light spread of his fingers to forbidden places, *dangerous* places, warming her insides. She took a step back, putting some distance between them.

The dress *was* provocative—the flesh revealed by the low neckline leaving a hint of the rounded curves of her breasts bare. It was more than she would normally put on display.

"It's one of Alexander's designs. He insisted I wear it tonight."

"I'm not surprised. It was made for you."

The sensual glitter in his eyes sent a skittering up her spine. Or maybe it was how good he looked in a silver-gray shirt and dark trousers that set off his spectacular dark coloring and beautiful eyes.

Her gaze dropped away from his. He curved his fingers around her jaw and brought it back up to his. The appraising look he subjected her to made her feel like glass—utterly transparent and far too vulnerable. "You've been off all day. What's wrong?"

She pulled free. "Nothing. I'm fine."

"No, you aren't." Irritation clouded his expression. "There's this thing that happens when we socialize, Angie. You turn into a plastic version of yourself. Aloof. Unreadable. Why?"

"That's hardly true."

"Every time, *cara*." He shoved his hands in his pockets and leaned back against the sill. "You can tell me or we can keep your parents waiting. It's all good with me."

Heat sizzled her blood. "Perhaps because it's always about a goal, a *business* transaction, rather than us enjoying ourselves. I was graded on my ability to accomplish those goals. Romance a partner of yours, flatter his wife, impress a potential target with my impeccable lineage..." She waved a hand at him. "Tonight it's Marc Bavaro—what's the goal with him? What would you like me to *be*, Lorenzo? Amusing? Intellectual? Cultured? Flirtatious?"

His gaze narrowed. "Not in that dress, no. And here we are getting somewhere, *bella mia. Communicating.* Because I had no idea you felt that pressure. *I* enjoy the thrill of the chase, accomplishing something by the end of the evening. To me it's us being a team. But I would *prefer* for you to be yourself...for you to be the woman I have always appreciated that never seems to show up on these occasions."

She leaned back against the sill, fingers curling around the edge. "And which woman is that? I'm intrigued despite myself, since I never seemed to get it right."

"The vibrant, spirited woman I met that night in Nassau who didn't seem to care what anyone else thought of her. Where has she gone, Angie? Where has that light gone?"

She blinked. Who did he think had snuffed out that spirit by asking her to be something she wasn't? By shutting her out when she displeased him? By constantly making her aware she wasn't measuring up?

She lifted her chin. "Why this sudden obsession with what makes me tick? It never seemed to concern you before."

"Perhaps because I'm realizing the woman I thought I knew has all these vulnerabilities lurking beneath the surface, vulnerabilities I think might be the key to why she is the way she is, and yet she won't let me near them."

"I think you're overthinking it."

"I think I'm not." He scowled and pulled his hands from his pockets. "I had some things to work through before, things I *have* worked on. It has proven illuminating to me. I would like to learn from it."

Things like Lucia? Her heart beat a jagged rhythm in her chest. To allow herself to believe that, to believe he truly cared, that he wanted to know her, *understand* her, that he truly wanted this time to be different between them, threatened to poke holes in the composure she desperately needed as she faced her old social set tonight. Not to mention her parents, who were waiting for them downstairs.

"We should go," she said quietly. "My parents will be waiting."

He pushed away from the sill. "We'll continue this later," he warned, setting a hand to the small of her back to guide her from the room. His warmth, his undeniable strength, bled into her skin. She swallowed hard. Somehow in the midst of all the chaos in her head, among all the conflicted feelings warring inside of her, his touch anchored her as it always had. Perhaps that was why it had hurt so much when he'd taken it away.

The poolside terrace was lit with flaming torches as they joined her parents outside, the lights from the sprawling, Italian-inspired villa reflected in the infinity pool that served as the star attraction of the space. Sleek waitstaff dressed in black hovered at the ready, the marble-and-brick bar stocked with rows of the perquisite champagne on ice.

Della and Alistair Carmichael were already

holding drinks, listening to the local band they'd hired to play. Angie gave her mother, who was looking her usual elegant self in a powder-blue cocktail dress, her silver-blond hair a perfect bob to her ears, a perfunctory kiss on the cheek. Her gaze slid down to the drink her mother held as she drew back, the tightness in her chest easing when she saw that it was sparkling water.

"You look beautiful, Mother."

"Thank you." Her mother gave her a critical once-over. "Faggini?"

"Yes." A wry smile twisted her lips at their practiced small talk. It was how they'd learned to co-exist after their fiery relationship during Angie's teenage years, when her mother's alcoholism had emerged and everything between them had been a war of wills. Their practiced détente still didn't quell the pain of losing the mother she'd once had, before Bella Carmichael's disease had devastated her, but at least it was a norm she knew how to maneuver within.

"Lorenzo." Her mother turned her attention to Angie's husband, the feminine smile she reserved for handsome, powerful men softening her face. "It's so lovely to see you." She kissed him on both cheeks. "Although," she said in a pointed tone as she drew back, "I think we've seen you more than our daughter over the past couple of years. Perhaps your reconciliation will remedy that."

"We're counting on it," her father said, stepping forward. Tall and distinguished with a hint of gray at his temples, his eyes were the same slate blue as his daughter's. That was where their similarities began and ended.

Eschewing the embrace he knew Angie would reject, he shook Lorenzo's hand. "Angelina knows how thrilled I am to see her back where she belongs."

Back where she belongs? A surge of antagonism pulsed through her. She wouldn't be in this situation if her father hadn't allowed his arrogance to blind him to the business realities staring him in the face. He was using her as a pawn and showed not the slightest conscience about it.

Lorenzo read the tension in her body, his palm tightening at her back. "My parents are in town next week," he said smoothly. "Perhaps you can join us for dinner? It would be nice for us all to reconnect."

Angie's back went ramrod-straight as her mother

gushed on about how lovely that would be. It wasn't lovely, it was the worst idea ever. To put Saint Octavia, Lorenzo's supremely dignified mother, in a room with her own, given Della Carmichael's loose-wheel status of late, was a recipe for disaster.

Thankfully they were saved from discussing it further as the first guests began to arrive.

Hand at his wife's back, Lorenzo greeted the arrivals. Guest after guest arrived in cars piloted by drivers who would spirit them from party to party that evening. His wife grew stiffer and stiffer with each new arrival and the open curiosity about their newly resurrected relationship. By the time Marc Bavaro, the CEO of the Belmont Hotel Group, arrived with his beautiful redheaded girlfriend, Penny, Angie had perfected her plastic self.

Lorenzo's inability to understand what was happening to her, as his need to connect on a personal level with Bavaro pressed on his brain, made his impatience boil over.

"That's Marc Bavaro and his girlfriend walking in now," he murmured in his wife's ear. "Can we try for happy just for the next few minutes?

Less like you're facing the executioner being by my side?"

Angelina pasted a smile on her face. "Of course," she said sweetly. "Your wish is my command."

Even without her real smile, his wife captivated Marc Bavaro. The CEO's leisurely once-over of Angelina's red dress, despite the stunning date at his side, made his wife's cheeks redden. So Marc Bavaro did have a roving eye, as advertised. Lorenzo couldn't necessarily blame him, given Angie's ability to mesmerize any red-blooded male with whom she came into contact.

He tightened his fingers around her waist. "Great that you could make it," he said to Marc. "Good to get out of the boardroom."

"Agreed." But Bavaro still wore the cagey expression that had been making Lorenzo mental as they debated the last few points of the deal.

"Your necklace is beautiful," Penny said to Angie. "Is it one of yours?"

"Yes. Thank you. It's one of my favorite recent pieces."

"I love your stuff." Penny threw Marc a wry glance. "I've given him lots of hints on what he can buy me for my birthday."

"Perhaps you'd like to come in to the studio and I'll design something for you?"

The redhead's eyes widened. "Would you?"

"Of course." Angelina slid Lorenzo a glance that said she was playing the game for now. "Why don't I introduce Penny around while you two talk business?"

Penny agreed and the two women set off through the crowd. Bavaro's eyes trailed after Angelina. "That's quite a dress."

"It is," Lorenzo agreed, amused. He didn't doubt the connection he and Angie had. It ruled out any other male as a threat. He was content to play the waiting game when it came to bedding his wife. Figuring out what was going on in her head was another matter entirely.

He nodded at Marc. "Let's find a quiet place to talk."

By the time Angie had introduced Penny around to anyone the real estate broker might have found interesting or useful, she'd had enough of this party for a lifetime. She hated small talk with a passion, had always dreaded the legendary Carmichael parties she'd been forced to attend, not to mention the fact that all roads seemed to lead back to her and Lorenzo's unexpected reconciliation in the sly side conversations she was drawn into.

"I thought maybe there was a baby in the works," joked their next-door neighbor. "But clearly that can't be true. That dress is *amazing* on you."

After the last, thinly veiled attempt to pry the story out of her, she returned Penny to Marc. The Belmont CEO asked her to dance in turn, and Penny didn't seem to mind, so Angie accepted, eager to get away from prying eyes. Marc was a good dancer and conversationalist. He was charming, despite Lorenzo's depiction of him as a shark.

They danced two dances before Lorenzo cut in. "I'm not sure if I should lock you up or use you as a weapon," he murmured as he took her in his arms. "Bavaro is like a puppy salivating after a bone."

"Ah, but I don't have a purpose tonight." Sarcasm stained her voice. "I'm just supposed to *be me* in all my glory. The woman you *appreciate*."

His lips curved. Bending his head, he brought his mouth to her ear. "I do appreciate you in that dress. It screams 'take me,' *mia cara*. Too bad we are still learning to communicate *verbally*. The timing is all off."

Fire licked up her spine. He pulled her closer, a possessive hand resting on her hip, his splayed fingers burning into her skin. A slow curl of heat unraveled inside of her. She'd enjoyed her dance with Marc—he was handsome by any woman's standards and equally charismatic. But being in Lorenzo's arms was a whole different story. Dancing with her husband was...*electrifying*.

Her nerve endings sizzled as her hips brushed against his muscular thighs, erotic tension in every muscle. The masculine warmth of him bled into her, heating her blood, weakening her knees. She took a deep breath to center herself, but it was his dark, delicious scent that filled her head, heightening her confusion.

She stepped back, putting some distance between them, heart thudding in her chest. His ebony eyes glittered with a banked heat, moving over her face in a silent study. "Thank you for offering to design the piece for Penny. You didn't have to do that."

"It's fine." The husky edge to her voice made

her wince. *You hate him, remember?* He had just turned her life upside down.

"Perhaps we will make that superior team," he suggested on a speculative note, eyes holding hers. "If you manage to move past that anger you're holding so tightly to."

Her gaze dropped away from his. She focused on the other guests, sticking determinedly to her vow to keep her shields bulletproof when it came to her husband.

A high-pitched laugh stole her attention. The blood in her veins turned to ice. Whipping her head around, she found her mother in the crowd, talking to a well-known society columnist, a glass of champagne in her hand. Oh, no! She'd found someone to enable her.

Panicked, she scanned the crowd for her sister. Abigail was all the way across the terrace in a group of people. She looked back at her mother, champagne sloshing from her glass as she laughed at something the columnist had said. It was not her first drink.

"Your mother is in fine form," Lorenzo said mildly.

Her brain frozen, she just stared at him. When

the music ended, she slipped out of his arms. "Keep socializing," she said, nodding at Marc. "Abigail's just waved for me to go meet someone."

He frowned at her. "Are you okay?"

"Perfect. Back in a minute." With as blasé a smile as she could manage, she set off through the crowd. Approaching the group her sister was in the middle of, she caught her eye. Abigail disentangled herself and came over. "You okay?"

"It's Mother. She has a glass of champagne in her hand. It's not her first."

Abigail frowned. "I've been watching her all night. She's been drinking sparkling water."

"She found someone to enable her." Angie's stomach lurched. "She's talking to Courtney Price, Abby."

Her sister's face grayed. Leading the way, Abigail wound her way through the crowd, Angie on her heels. Her mother had drained the champagne and procured another glass by the time they reached her. Her loud voice penetrated the din of the crowd, drawing glances from those around her. Angie's heart plummeted.

"You grab her," Abigail muttered. "Get her out of here. I'll do damage control."

Angie nodded. Heart in her mouth, she headed toward her glassy-eyed mother. Her mother glared at her. "Oh, look!" she declared in that far too loud tone. "My daughters are here to cut me off before I say something I shouldn't. I haven't, have I, Courtney? We're just having a nice conversation."

Courtney Price had a half fascinated, half horrified look on her face. *Brilliant column fodder.* Angie reached for her mother's arm. "Actually I have someone I'd like you to meet."

Her mother yanked back her arm. The force of the movement sent the champagne flying from her glass, splattering the dress of the woman beside her. Paralyzed, Angie stared at the silk dress, then lifted her gaze to the woman's bemused face. She was the wife of one of Lorenzo's business acquaintances.

Oh, hell.

Gasps rang out around her. The shocked sounds spurred her into action. Grabbing her mother by the arm, she propelled her through the crowd, people gawking at them as they went. Angry and humiliated, her mother kept up a verbal barrage the whole way.

"It was *your* fault that happened, hauling me out of there like that."

Angie kept her mouth shut. Nodding her thanks at the butler who opened the patio door for them, she marched her mother inside and up the stairs toward her parents' suite, keeping her mother's weaving steps on course. Where the hell was her father? Somehow this just never seemed to be his job.

Guiding her mother inside her suite, she flicked on the light. Her mother stared at her belligerently, hands on her hips. "All I wanted was to have some fun," she said, her speech slurred. "All I wanted was to be *happy* tonight, Angelina. But you won't even give me that."

A lump formed in her throat. "You're an alcoholic, Mother. You can't drink. *Ever.*"

"I am fine." Her mother put her arms out as she lost her balance and weaved to the side. "I would have been fine. I only had a couple of drinks."

A lie. Angie had heard so many of them, about the drinking, about the pills, about every secret her mother had wanted to hide—it had become her normal state of being.

Her mother headed toward the bar in the lounge.

Threw open the door of the fridge. "There's nothing in there," Angie said quietly, stomach churning. "You need to go back for treatment, Mother. You know that."

Her mother swung around. Fear pierced her hazel eyes. "I told Abigail I won't go back there. *Ever. Never* again."

"You need help. Professional help."

"I won't go."

"Yes, you will." Rage vibrated through her. "You will not destroy all of us in your quest to annihilate yourself. Abigail needs a life. *I* need a life. You need help."

"You," her mother said, fixing her with a vicious look. *"You* who don't care. You who turned your back on me and walked away."

"Because I couldn't stand it anymore. Because you were taking me apart piece by piece, Mother."

Her mother's gaze darkened. She pressed her fingers to her mouth. "I don't feel well."

Angie moved fast, sliding an arm around her and helping her to the bathroom. When her mother had upended the contents of her stomach multiple times, Angie cleaned her up and put her to bed.

"I'm sorry." Her mother started to cry, her transformation from angry to sad happening with its usual rapid-fire swiftness. "I'm so sorry."

Heat burned the back of Angelina's eyes, the pieces of her heart she'd finally healed shattering all over again. "I know." She clasped her mother's hand in hers, hot tears escaping her stinging eyes and sliding down her face. "I am, too."

For everything. For all of it.

Turning off the light, she let herself out of the room. Tears blinding her vision, knees shaking, she slid down the other side of the door until she sat on the floor, hands pressed to her face.

She couldn't do this again.

CHAPTER FIVE

"ANGELINA?" LORENZO PULLED to a halt when he saw his wife sitting in the hallway, legs drawn up, head in her hands. Her quiet sobs tore loose a piece of his heart.

He squatted down beside her. "What's wrong?"

No response. He tipped her face up to his. "Angelina," he said more urgently, "what happened?"

Her beautiful blue eyes were red-stained, unfocused. Heart jamming in his throat, he cupped her jaw. "*Dio*, Angie. Talk to me. What's wrong?"

She shook her head as if to clear it. Lifted a hand to push her hair out of her face. "I—" Another tear streaked down her cheek.

He cursed. Slid his arms beneath her knees and back and scooped her off the floor. Carrying her down the hallway to their suite, he shouldered the door open and set her on the sofa in the sitting room. Her beautiful red dress was wet, stained with something. Champagne, he assumed, from the story he'd heard.

He sat down beside her. "What the hell happened out there?"

She frowned. Rubbed a palm over her brow. "I'm so sorry about Magdalena's dress. Did Abigail smooth it over?"

"Magdalena's dress will survive. What the hell happened with your mother, Angie?"

Her gaze slid away from his. "She had a bit too much to drink."

His brow rose. "She was drunk. *Blotto.* She could hardly stand up. I'd say it was more than a bit too much."

She bit her lip. "So she was drunk. It happens. I apologize for the scene she caused."

"I don't care about the scene." A flash of heat consumed him. "I just found my wife crumpled in a ball in the hallway crying her eyes out... *Dio mio*, Angelina, what is going on?"

Her chin dipped. "It's nothing. I'm just...emotional. It's been a tough night."

He pulled in a breath. Counted to five. "You can either tell me why you've been such a disaster tonight, what is going on with your family, or I will go outside and ask Abigail. In the spirit of making our relationship work, I'd prefer, however, if the truth came from *my wife*."

She stared at him for a long time. He held her gaze, ready to follow through on his threat.

"My mother is a functioning alcoholic," she said finally. "She's been that way since I was fifteen. We've managed to keep it from being public knowledge, have taken her to rehab twice, each time thinking it would be the last. This recent dry spell lasted two years. She started to slide backward when the money troubles began."

A red tide swept through him. "You were carrying this around with you our entire marriage and you didn't tell me?"

"My mother swore us to secrecy. It was the only way she'd agree to go for treatment. It was decided it would remain locked within the walls of the Carmichael family vault. If we didn't speak of it, didn't acknowledge it, it ceased to exist."

He frowned. "Who *decided* this?"

"My father."

"I'm assuming your sister's husband doesn't know, then, either?"

A flush swept her cheeks.

"*Dannazione*, Angelina." His hands clenched into fists by his sides. "Why didn't you feel you could trust me with this?"

She waved a hand at him. "You have the perfect family, Lorenzo. I was worried you would look down on us. You have such a disdain for a lack of discipline."

Heat seared his skin. "I would have *helped* you, not looked down on you. That's what a husband and wife do for each other."

"And we had that aspect of our relationship perfected, didn't we?" Her eyes flashed. "I never felt good enough for you, Lorenzo. Appreciated by you. *Ever*. Not after those first few months when you started tuning me out. Treating me like an afterthought. At least when you wanted me, I felt I had some value. When you lost interest in even that, it *decimated* me. Why would I tell you about my mother? Air my family's dirty laundry? All that would have done was make you regret your decision to marry me even more."

"I did *not* regret my decision to marry you. *Ever*." He stared at her, stunned. "Is that what you think?"

No response.

Confusion warred with fury, the red tide in him winning. "You are so off base, Angelina. *So* off base. I might have been distant, we agree that I was, but do you really think I would have thought any less of you because of this? That I wouldn't have supported you?"

Her mouth pursed. "I don't know."

His breath hissed from his lungs. His marriage was suddenly illuminated in a way it had never been before. What the cost of his emotional withdrawal had been on his wife. What he should have *seen*. He didn't like what he saw.

He took hold of her hand and pulled her to her feet. Turning her around, he reached for the zipper of her dress. She jerked away from him, eyes wide. "What are you doing?"

"Putting you to bed."

"I can't go to *bed*. The party's still going."

He moved his gaze over her face. "You're a mess. You can't go back down there. Things are winding down, anyway. I'll go finish up."

He turned her around and slid down the zipper. She pulled away, arms crossed over her chest. "I can do the rest."

He headed for the door. "Did Abby talk to

Courtney Price?" she called after him. "She can't print this in her column tomorrow."

He turned around. "She pulled her aside. I saw them talking."

Her face relaxed. "Abby will fix it. She always does."

Abby will fix it. She always does. The words rang in his head as Lorenzo went back to the party. Is that what Angelina and her sister had spent the past decade doing? Fixing their mother's lapses before they made it to the tabloids? Preserving a family secret that was tearing his wife apart, a secret he hadn't known about because he'd been too caught up in himself, in his own stuff, to see the warning signals?

The tension that had always lain between his wife and her parents, the distance she'd put between herself and them this past couple of years, his wife's refusal to ever have more than one or two drinks no matter what was put in front of her—it all made sense now.

Anger at his own blindness fueling him, he found Alistair Carmichael and ensured he went and checked on his wife. What kind of a man was he to leave it to his daughters to pick up the pieces? To ignore what was clearly a cry for help from his wife?

Perhaps, he thought, the same kind of man *he* had been during his marriage. A man who had simply not been there.

Angie willed herself to sleep after Lorenzo left, curling up into a ball under the cool satin sheets and squeezing her eyes shut. But the scene with her mother kept replaying itself over and over again in her head.

You who don't care. You who turned your back and walked away.

A knot tied itself in her stomach. She *had* walked away. Because going through what had happened tonight again and again, never reaching that place inside of her mother that was in so much pain she couldn't heal, had taken a piece of her soul.

She burrowed into the pillow, an ache consuming her insides. Lorenzo's anger, his *fury*, twisted the knot tighter. Perhaps she should have told him. Perhaps she was as guilty of holding things inside as he was. Except it was difficult to communicate with a brick wall and that's what he'd been near the end.

She hugged the pillow tighter. Tried to force herself to sleep, because it hurt too much to be in the here and now. But she couldn't settle. She was still awake when Lorenzo came in just after one, stripped off his clothes, showered and came to bed.

He smelled so good, so achingly real and familiar, she had to fight the urge to beg him to hold her. Closing her eyes, she curled her fingers into the sheets. Lorenzo sighed, reached for her and turned her toward him. Feeling utterly exposed with her tearstained face and puffy eyes, she closed her eyes.

He ran a finger down her cheek, making her lashes flutter open. "Angie," he murmured, "*mia cara*. Things between us have to change. You have to learn to trust me. I have to get better at reading you…at knowing when you need me, because clearly I am terrible at that."

She searched the angular shadows of his face in the moonlight. "You're serious about this."

"You think I would have done what I've done if I wasn't? I want you back because you are meant to be with me, Angie, not because I have some cruel desire to make you suffer. I *married* you because you are beautiful and intelligent, because you were what *I* wanted in a wife, not simply because you were pregnant. Because for the first time since Lucia died, I felt alive. *You* made me feel alive."

Her heart stuttered in her chest. If she had sensed that this was the case, felt that intense connection that had bonded them together, he had never once verbalized it. When he had begun to shut her out, she'd convinced herself she'd imagined it, that she was delusional and hopelessly naive where he was concerned. But this, *this*, she didn't know how to process.

His fingers traced the edge of her jaw, commanding her attention. "If we had disagreements about how our relationship worked, it didn't mean I found you *lacking*—it meant we had issues to resolve. To say we didn't do a very good job of that is an understatement."

She bit her lip, the salt tang of blood filling her mouth. She'd been convinced he'd wanted her because she'd been a politically viable Carmichael, as a wife who could open doors for him in alternate social circles. For what he'd *thought* he'd been signing on for. If it really had been more than that, if he had wanted her for *her*, what did that mean?

Had she walked out on a marriage that had been reparable if she'd just stuck? It was an overwhelming, earth-shattering prospect to consider. She sucked in a deep breath and lifted her gaze to his. "Every time you withdrew I felt it as a rejection. It hurt, Lorenzo, badly."

"I know. I realize that now."

A long moment passed. His fingers slid to her cheek, thumb tracing over the tracks of her tears. The ache inside her grew until it was almost all-encompassing. The need for everything they'd had. Everything they'd never had. For this to be different this time as he was promising it would be. But she didn't know if she could trust him, wasn't sure she could go through another of his Jekyll-and-Hyde routines. Didn't know if she could trust her *own* instincts anymore.

Fear invaded her, coiled its way around her insides. She pushed a hand into the mattress to move before she did something she would regret. Something she wasn't ready for. Before she *did* beg him to hold her. Lorenzo hooked an arm around her waist and tucked her into the warmth of his body before she could, her back nestled against his chest. "Go to sleep," he murmured, brushing his lips over her shoulder in a fleeting caress. "Tomorrow we'll deal with what happens next."

Except she couldn't relax. Couldn't slow down her brain. Not with him so close, clad only in the sexy hipster briefs he'd added to his routine in deference to their *adjustment period*. Not when tomorrow would mean deciding what to do with her mother. Convincing her to go back to the treatment facility in California she swore she wouldn't return to.

Silent tears slid down her face. She reached up to brush them away, shocked there were any left. Lorenzo muttered an oath. *"Don't,"* he murmured, shifting so she lay back against the pillows. "We're going to solve this—I promise."

She should have protested when he set his mouth to her jaw. As he kissed and licked away her tears, working his way up one cheek, then down the other. But the erotic, soul-searing comfort he offered eased the ache inside of her. Lit her up in a way only Lorenzo could.

A low sound escaped her throat. Her eyes locked

with his in a hot, heated moment that held time suspended. Murmuring her name, he closed his mouth over hers, taking her lips in a slow, sweet kiss that drove everything from her head but him. How much she missed this. How much she missed everything about it.

He captured her jaw in his fingers, held her as he dipped deeper into her mouth, his tongue sliding against hers. The taste of him exploded through her, dark and dangerous as she tangled her legs with his, a tight fist of need forming in her stomach. She twisted closer, seeking, *needing* the oblivion he could give her because this, *this* had always been right.

She rocked against him. His obvious arousal, covered only by the thin cotton briefs, sank into her softness, the delicate material of her panties no obstacle. She gasped as he moved against her with possessive intent, the friction turning her insides molten.

"Lorenzo..."

He threaded a hand through her hair, held her still as he lifted his mouth from hers. "Angie," he murmured softly. "No."

No? Her eyes flew open.

"You will hate me tomorrow, *cara*. I guarantee it. You're emotional. I won't take advantage of that."

Her brain right-sided itself with a swiftness that made her dizzy. She pushed a hand against his chest, humiliation and confusion flaming through her. Lorenzo levered himself off of her. She scrambled to the other side of the bed, pressing her hands against her cheeks. "You started it."

"I wanted to comfort you," he said softly. "It got out of hand."

She turned her back on him and curled up in a ball.

"Angie." He laid a hand on her shoulder.

"Leave me alone." She took a deep breath as her fractured breathing slowed. She had no idea what she was doing. Thinking. Nothing made sense anymore. Everything she'd thought was true was now a massive gray area she had no idea what to do with.

Pain throbbed at the back of her eyes, her heart a rock in her throat. Lorenzo was just as much of an addiction for her as the alcohol her mother consumed. Just as dangerous. She would do well to remember that before she started making life-changing, potentially disastrous decisions to sleep with him again. Her husband was right in that.

She closed her eyes. This time sleep came swift and hard with the need to escape.

CHAPTER SIX

ANGIE WOKE THE next morning heavy-headed and bleary-eyed. Apprehensive about what lay ahead, confused about what had happened between her and Lorenzo last night, she dressed in jeans and a tunic, threw her hair into a ponytail and headed downstairs to the breakfast room, hoping it would be empty so she could spend a few minutes composing herself over coffee.

Her wish was not to be granted. Her husband sat by himself in the sun-filled room that overlooked the bay, the morning's newspapers spread out in front of him. He looked gorgeous in jeans and a navy T-shirt, his thick, dark hair still wet and slicked back from his shower. It was utterly disconcerting the way her heart quickened at the sight of him, as if it had a mind of its own.

He looked up, gaze sliding over her face. "You slept in. That's good. You needed it."

She took a seat beside him at the head of the

table, even though her brain was screaming for distance. It would have looked churlish to do otherwise.

"Constanza made your favorite," he said, waving an elegant, long-fingered hand at the freshly baked banana bread on a plate. "And the coffee's hot."

"Thank you." She poured herself a cup of coffee. "Where are my parents?"

"Your father went for a run. Your mother's still in bed."

And would be for a while, she figured, taking a sip of the hot, delicious coffee. His brow furrowed. "Your father, he is always this...*distant* when it comes to dealing with your mother?"

"Always. He thinks she is weak. That she should be able to conquer this addiction. When she slips it infuriates him."

"That's no way to get to the heart of the problem. Your mother needs support above all things."

She eyed him. "You were the king of distancing yourself when I displeased you."

"Yes," he agreed, dark gaze flickering. "And we've talked about how I'm going to work on that."

Right. And she was just supposed to take that at

surface value? Forget the big stretches of complete alienation that had passed between them when he'd retreated into that utterly unknowable version of himself? How every time they'd made up in bed she'd thought it would be *better* just like she'd thought it would be better every time her mother promised to stop drinking, only to discover nothing had really changed.

She twisted her cup in its saucer. "It's always been that way in my family. We are the exact opposite of the Riccis—instead of expressing our emotions we bury them. Instead of talking about things we pretend they don't exist."

He frowned. "Ignoring an addiction, continuing to perpetuate an illusion that everything is fine when it isn't, is inherently damaging to all involved."

"I told you my family is dysfunctional."

The furrow in his brow deepened. "You said your mother started drinking when you were fifteen. What do you think precipitated it?"

She lifted a shoulder. "She always had the tendency to drink to cope with all the socializing. But I think it was my father's affairs that did it. Ask her to represent the family three or four times a week—fine. Ask her to do that when everyone is talking about who my father is screwing that week...to suffer that humiliation? It was too much."

"Why didn't she leave him?"

"She's a Carmichael. Image is everything. A Carmichael never concedes defeat. *Ever.* If we don't get her help, she will drink herself into the ground proving she can make this marriage work."

"That's nuts."

She arched a brow. "Didn't you say there's never been a Ricci divorce? It's what our families do."

He sat back in his chair, a contemplative look on his face. "That's why you don't like this world. Why you hate parties like the one we had last night. You hate what they represent."

"Yes."

"So you decided to leave me so you would never end up like your mother. You crave independence because you need to have an escape route in case our marriage falls apart like your parents' did."

Her mouth twisted. "That's far too simplistic an analysis."

"Perhaps, but I think your experiences drove your thinking with us. My withdrawal from you evoked shades of your father. Leaving you alone to cope while I went off to manage an empire. Except my vice wasn't other women, it was my work."

Her lashes lowered. "There may be some truth in that. But *saying* you're going to be more present and doing it are two different things."

"True," he conceded. "We can start with your mother, then."

"That's my issue to handle."

"No," he disagreed. "It's *our* issue. Like I said last night, we are going to handle this together. As a team. The way we should have the first time. You are not alone in this."

She shook her head. "It gets messy with my mother. It will be awkward for you."

"Exactly why I should be there." His jaw was a stubborn, unyielding line. "I saw you last night, Angie, crumpled on the floor. You were a wreck. This isn't going to be easy for you."

She pushed a hand through her hair. "You want to solve this like you want to solve everything, Lorenzo. Snap your fingers and *poof*, it's fixed. But it's far more complex than that."

"I know that. That's why the power of two will be better than one."

She exhaled a breath and stared out at the water, sparkling in the sun like the most electric of blue jewels. "We need to convince her to go back to the treatment facility in California. She's refusing to go."

"I may have an option. I called a friend of mine this morning. He had a brother in a facility in upstate New York that's supposed to be a leading edge program. If your mother was closer, perhaps it wouldn't be so difficult for her. You could visit her more often."

Her throat locked. The visits to see her mother in rehab had been the worst. Angry, bitter Della Carmichael had not gone easy despite recognizing the help she was getting. To put herself through even more of that with regular visits? The coward in her shrank from the idea, but she was starting to realize running from her problems hadn't gotten her anywhere—not with her mother and not with her marriage.

"We could go see it," her husband offered. "Then you can decide."

She eyed him. Her husband wanted to solve her

problem because it was just one more obstacle be-tween him and what he wanted—a wife able to devote her full attention to him. And yet, when he had comforted her last night she could have sworn he truly cared. That she meant something to him.

Perhaps she needed to exhibit a show of faith in them if this was going to work—a tiny, baby step forward, with her head firmly on her shoulders, of course. Last night had proven the need for that.

"All right," she said. "Let's go see it."

Angie and Lorenzo flew to upstate New York the next morning and met with the staff of the treat-ment center. Nestled in the foothills of the Adiron-dacks, the setting was lovely. By the time they'd finished touring the facility and meeting with the staff and doctors, Angie had an immediate com-fort level with it.

They flew her mother up there to see it later in the week. If Della approved of the choice, the center could take her immediately. Surprisingly, her mother liked it. Angie's emotions were torn to shreds by the time her mother cycled through the anger and sadness that was her pattern before agreeing to stay. But, somehow, with Lorenzo at her side, it wasn't as much of a nightmare as she'd expected. Her husband was endlessly patient with her mother, commanding when he needed to be, caring when Della required a softer touch. Where had this man been, she wondered, during their marriage?

By the time they'd boarded the jet, headed for home, she felt numb.

"You okay?" Lorenzo looked at her from the seat beside her, his laptop conspicuously absent on the console.

She nodded. "I hate leaving her there. Please let this be the last time we have to do this."

He closed his fingers over hers. "Hopefully it is. If it's not, we'll keep doing it until she's better. You're strong, Angie. You can do this."

She looked down at his hand curved around hers. Warm and protective, as he'd been all day. Her confusion heightened until it was that thick gray cloud, blanketing her brain. "Thank you," she murmured huskily, "for being there for me this week. I swore I'd never do this again because it hurts too much. But I'm learning running doesn't solve anything."

"No, it doesn't," he agreed, eyes darkening. "But

sometimes we need to do things in our own time. Allow ourselves the space to heal."

Lucia. He was talking about Lucia again. A tight knot formed in her stomach. She couldn't ignore it any longer—this ghost that had always lain between them. She knew it was at the heart of figuring them out.

She pulled her hand out from under his. "What you said the night before the party—that you had worked through some things. Was one of them Lucia?"

A guarded expression moved across his face. "Yes. When I met you, I thought I had moved on, gotten through the worst of the grieving process. But after you left, I realized I hadn't left that process behind as fully as I'd imagined. That perhaps I had carried some of that baggage into our marriage—baggage which did make me emotionally unavailable at times."

She frowned. "You told me it was *my* issue with Lucia that was the problem."

His mouth twisted. "Because you made me furious. Pointing fingers at the ghost of Lucia was your favorite card to play when you were angry with me, *cara.*"

Her eyelids lowered. She couldn't deny that. She'd lashed out in whatever way she could to get a response out of him. Something, *anything* to show he'd cared. She'd known it was wrong to use Lucia as a weapon against him, but their fights hadn't exactly been rational ones.

"Tell me about her," she said quietly. "Tell me about what happened. I need to understand, Lorenzo. Maybe if I had, things would have been different."

He sat back. Rubbed a palm against his temple. "Where to start? Lucia and I were childhood sweethearts. We spent the summers together in Lake Como. Eventually our childhood crush developed into an adult romance. Our families were all for it, it seemed...*predestined*, in a way."

Her stomach clenched. She had felt that way about him when they'd met, their connection had been so strong, so immediate. But Lorenzo's heart had belonged to someone else.

"We didn't marry right away," he continued. "I needed to sow my wild oats. I wasn't sure I could marry the first girl I fell in love with. But after a few years, I knew it was her. We married when I was twenty-six. I was in New York by then, she joined me here." His dark lashes arced over his cheeks. "She was like a fish out of water, missing her family, missing Italy. I did the best I could to make her happy. She kept saying once she had a baby, once we started a family, everything would change. We were trying for that when she…"

Died. Her chest seized tight. She curled her fingers over his. "It's okay. You don't have to talk about it."

"No—you're right. You need to know what happened. It's…a part of me." He palmed his jaw, dragging his fingers over dark stubble. "The incident at the town house happened when I was in Shanghai on business. We had an excellent security system there. Impenetrable—like the one we have now. But the men who broke in were professionals—*violent* professionals. They knew how to talk their way into someone's home, knew the stories to tell. Lucia was so innocent—she never stood a chance."

Her stomach curled in on itself. "She let them in."

He nodded. "They put her in my den. Told her to stay there while they went and cleaned out the place. They left her alone for a few moments and she called for help on her cell. One of them came back, saw what she was doing and hit her with the blunt end of the gun." His fingers flexed on his thigh, his knuckles gleaming white. "The blow to the head caused a severe bleed on her brain. She never regained consciousness."

Angie pressed her fingers to her mouth in horror. "How do you know all of this?" she whispered.

"Surveillance video."

Her stomach dropped, a sick feeling twisting her gut. "Please tell me you didn't watch it."

"I had to. I had to know what happened."

The raspy note in his voice, the raw emotion in his dark eyes, tore a piece of her heart loose. What would it do to a person to go through that? To lose someone you love like that? It would change you forever.

"I'm sorry," she said quietly, a sinking feeling settling through her for all the wrongs they'd done each other. "For being so insensitive. I knew what happened to Lucia was horrible. I knew I should make allowances for it. But every time you retreated, every time you turned off, I hurt so badly, I just wanted you to hurt like I was hurting. It became instinctual, *reflexive*. But it didn't make it right."

He shook his head. "We were *both* experts at slinging arrows. It became easier than dealing with what was in front of us."

She caught her lip between her teeth. Stared out the window at a sea of blue, her ragged emotions begging her to stop. But to do that would stall them where they stood, suspended in a state of perpetual animation. It would not *fix* them.

"I know Lucia will always be in your heart," she said quietly when she turned back to him. "I wouldn't expect any less. The issue between us was the emotional distance it caused, the emotional distance you put between us. I need to know you are over her, Lorenzo."

His cheeks hollowed. "I have let her go. I have moved on. That's what this is all about, Angelina—moving forward. I'm asking you to do that with me."

Her chest went tight. She knew they needed to let go of the past if they were going to make this work. But could she do it? Could she trust her instincts where Lorenzo was concerned? Could she trust that he had changed? Or was she setting herself up for an even greater fall than she'd taken the first time?

"Maybe what we need," he said quietly, a contemplative look on his face, "is a fresh start. A blank slate. No ghosts, no animosity, just us."

Her heart contracted on a low, painful pull. It was so tempting to believe they could recapture the good they'd had. That she could claim that piece of his heart she'd always craved. Because when it had been good between them, it had been good in a way nothing else could touch. And when it had been bad, he had eviscerated her.

Blood pumped through her veins, her breath caught in her throat. Suddenly her baby steps seemed like a heart-pumpingly, scary big leap.

"All of you," Lorenzo said evenly, eyes on hers. "That's what I'm asking for. A real shot at this. Can you give me that?"

She swallowed past a paper-dry throat. Took the leap. "I can try."

Lorenzo put his emotionally exhausted wife to bed after a light dinner, then headed to his study to work. The logistics with Angelina's mother had taken a big bite out of his week. He was behind and his inability to connect with Marc Bavaro, who had disappeared on a multiweek trip to South America, meant the acquisition was still in limbo.

Resisting the temptation to drown his frustration in a potent shot of something strong because it would also dull his brain with hours of work ahead of him, he fixed himself a cappuccino in Constanza's steel marvel of a kitchen, returned to his study and picked up a report he had to review before his morning meeting, but the numbers blurred before his eyes.

His thoughts were consumed, instead, by his wife's haunted face as he'd put her to bed. With the fact that he had clearly never known her. Far from being the spoiled young woman he'd thought he'd married who was incapable of compromise, she was instead a vulnerable, emotional woman he'd never looked deep enough to see. A woman who had gone through hell under the purview of parents who had, in reality, been nothing of the sort.

That his wife had been strong enough at fifteen to police her mother at parties, to keep up a facade for as long as she and Abigail had, to take her mother to rehab not once but *twice*, by the time she was twenty, little more than a girl herself, boggled his mind. It was courage on a scale he couldn't imagine. Made him feel as if he'd just taken a hard shot to the solar plexus.

He sat back in his chair and closed his eyes, guilt twisting his insides. Twice now he'd failed to react when the most important women in his life had cried out for help. Failed to recognize what they'd been trying to tell him. *Failed to protect them*.

It shamed him on the most visceral of levels, raked across the dark presence that seemed to lurk just beneath the surface of his skin, searching for a way to the top.

Angie had always believed Lucia had his heart, that he wasn't over her and that was what had caused him to hold back with her. Instead the truth was something far worse. If he'd listened to Lucia, if he'd been *present* for her as Angelina liked to cite as his greatest fault, then she would still be alive.

Agitation drove him to his feet and to the window, where he stood looking out at a floodlit view of Central Park. The darkness pressed against his edges—relentless, *hungry*. He would never forgive himself for what had happened to Lucia because he didn't deserve it. But he could do things differently with Angelina this time.

He pressed a palm against his temple. If there was guilt for not being able to give his wife the love she so clearly craved, *deserved*, the love she'd never been shown, he would have to appease himself with the promise he would give her everything else. He would *be there* for her this time.

Because to allow his marriage to descend into the emotionally addictive union it had once been? To allow himself to feel the things for Angelina he once had? To experience more loss? Not happening.

Emotion had destroyed them the first time around, rationality and practicality would save them. That and the combustible chemistry he had slammed the breaks on in the Hamptons.

The lush, heady, spellbindingly feminine taste of his wife as she'd begged him to take her filled his head. He wanted to dull the edge, kill the need that drove him whenever he was within five feet of her. With a clean slate ahead of them, an agreement from Angelina to leave their ghosts behind them, he intended to accomplish that goal in short order.

He *would* have his delectable wife back in his bed, in every sense of the word. Would make this marriage into what it always should have been.

CHAPTER SEVEN

"DAMN." ANGIE SCOOPED the bracelet off the bedroom floor and attempted to refasten it around her wrist. She had been late coming home from the studio, where she'd been putting the final touches on Faggini's collection, which would debut at Fashion Week next week, not an ideal night to be running behind with Lorenzo's parents coming for dinner.

The clasp slipped from her fingers *again*. She grimaced. Was she that unnerved by the thought of a visit from Octavia the Great or did it have more to do with the fact she'd agreed to give her marriage a real shot? She suspected it was a combination of both.

"Need help?" Lorenzo emerged from the dressing area, rolling up the sleeves of the crisp white shirt he'd put on.

"Yes." She handed him the bracelet. "Please."

He slid it around her wrist, making quick work

of the clasp. His gaze met hers. "Are you stressing about tonight? You have to stop doing that. Everyone wants us to work, including my parents."

"I'm not stressed, I'm late."

"You're not late. They're not even here yet."

He slid an arm around her waist and tugged her close. Smoking hot in dark pants and the white shirt, he made her heart thud in her chest. "I appreciate the fact that they are late, however," he drawled, "since I have not had time to greet you properly."

Her stomach clenched, heat radiating through her insides. He had a distinctly predatory look in his eyes tonight, one that suggested their adjustment period was officially over.

"Your parents will be arriving any minute,"

"Plenty of time." He slid his fingers into her hair, cupped her scalp and kissed her. A long, slow shimmer of a connection, it was leisurely and easy, a magic dancing in the air between them that stole her breath. Her palms settled on his chest, grabbed handfuls of shirt as her knees melted beneath her.

"Lorenzo," she murmured when they came up

for air, "you are ruining my hair, not to mention my lipstick."

"Mmm." He slid his mouth across her jaw, down to the hollow of her throat. Pressed his lips to her pulse. It was racing like a jackhammer, revealing every bit of the tumult raging inside of her. He flicked his tongue across the frantic beat, his palms clamping on her hips to draw her closer.

He was all hard, solid muscle beneath her hands. The most exciting man on earth to her—always had been. She swayed closer, molding herself to his hard contours. He returned his attention to her mouth, each nip countered by a soothing lave of his tongue over tender flesh.

Drowning. She was drowning.

The doorbell rang. Jolted out of her pheromone-induced haze, Angie stiffened and dragged herself out of his arms. Lorenzo watched her with a satisfied look as he straightened his shirt. "Now you look like a proper wife."

She ignored him, walked to the mirror to straighten her hair and reapply her lipstick. It took several deep pulls of air to get her breath back. Her equilibrium.

Hand at her back, he guided her out to the foyer,

where Constanza was greeting his parents. Lorenzo shook his father's hand, kissed his mother's cheeks, then drew Angie forward. She opted for the less threatening target first, Lorenzo's father, Salvatore.

Graying at the temples, shorter than his son by a couple of inches and stockier in middle age, Salvatore Ricci had always been much more approachable than his wife despite his fearsome business reputation.

"Buonasera, Angelina," he murmured, bending to brush a kiss against both of her cheeks. *"È bello rivederti."*

It's good to see you again. She forced a smile to her lips. *"Altrettanto."*

She turned to Lorenzo's mother, perfectly turned out as usual in an eggplant silk wrap dress that came to the knee and sleek Italian heels on her dainty feet. With her short, silver hair and her son's dark, dark eyes, she was still a stunningly beautiful woman. *"Buonasera, Octavia."*

"Buonasera." Octavia brushed a kiss to both her cheeks. "Thank you for having us."

"It's so lovely you are in town." Angie summoned the perfect manners she'd been taught since birth as she ushered Lorenzo's parents into the salon and offered them a drink. She had bemoaned all those social niceties as a teenager, finding them false and disingenuous, but right now, in this moment, she was exceedingly glad to have them to fall back upon.

It seemed everyone was on their best behavior as they enjoyed a cocktail before dinner. Lorenzo kept a palm to her back, a protective gesture Angie welcomed. Octavia didn't miss it, her shrewd dark eyes moving between the two of them every so often as if to assess what the real truth of them was.

Angie told herself she wasn't that twenty-two-year-old girl who'd been hopelessly intimidated by her mother-in-law. She was a successful business owner, every bit a match for Octavia Ricci. The thought settled her nerves as she sat beside Lorenzo at the table on the terrace Constanza had set with an elegant candelabra blazing in the final, hazy light of day. Lorenzo's parents sat opposite them, the humidity-free night a perfect choice for dinner outside.

The wine flowed freely, as did the conversation.

By the time their salad plates were cleared, Angie had begun to relax, if not enjoy herself.

Octavia set her gaze on her daughter-in-law. "Lorenzo tells me you're partnering with Alexander Faggini on his show. That's impressive."

"Providing the jewelry," Angie amended carefully. "Alexander is the star. But yes, thank you, it's very exciting. Would you like to come?"

Octavia frowned. "We have dinner plans." She turned to her husband. "We could move them, couldn't we?"

"I'm sure that won't be a problem. It would be fun for you."

"Bene." Octavia flashed one of her queen-like smiles. "I would love to, then. Is your mother coming?"

Her heart skipped a beat. "I'm afraid not. She's out of town."

"Oh, that's too bad." Her mother-in-law looked anything but sad. "Where is she?"

"The south of France with family." She gave the cover she and Abigail had agreed on.

Octavia wrinkled her nose. "Isn't it *hot* there this time of year? I can't wait to escape the heat in the summer."

"We have a house there. She loves the flowers in the summer."

"I see."

"You must come with Lorenzo the next time he's in Italy," Salvatore inserted. "It would be nice for you to reconnect with the family."

"That would be lovely." She had no intention, however, of putting herself in the midst of Lorenzo's big, gregarious family until she and her husband had proven they could make this work. "It may be next year, I'm afraid. As soon as Fashion Week is over I'll be ramping up for the Christmas season. Things will be crazy right through January."

"I expect," Octavia interjected smoothly, "you will have to scale back once you and Lorenzo are expecting. My son tells me the pace you've been working at. That can't be good for a pregnancy."

Angie stiffened. Shot a sideways look at her husband. "Lorenzo and I are taking our time with that. But I see no reason not to keep working. I think it's healthier for a woman to stick to her usual lifestyle."

"Yes," said Octavia, "but it's common knowledge women who work too much have more difficulty conceiving. They are more stressed and the process doesn't happen so easily."

The *process* hadn't even happened between her and Lorenzo yet... How dare Octavia interfere like this? Lips pursed, she picked up her wine and took a sip. Lorenzo set a palm on her thigh.

"Give us time, Mamma. Angie and I have just reconciled. There will be plenty of opportunities to make babies."

"Angie is approaching twenty-six," Octavia countered. "You may need time."

Blood rushed to her cheeks. They were discussing her like she was a broodmare. Completely disregarding the fact that she wasn't *ready* to get pregnant, as her career was at a critical juncture. Or that she had miscarried the last time she had carried Lorenzo's baby, a soul-clawing experience she never wanted to repeat again. Not to mention the fact that her husband had shut down emotionally afterward, the impetus to the end of their marriage.

Lorenzo set a hard stare on his mother. "We had no problems conceiving before. We're not in any rush."

His mother lifted an elegant shoulder. "Angie

was young then—at the prime of her fertility. I'm simply giving you my advice. Women think they can wait forever these days and it just doesn't happen that way."

Angie drew in a breath. Lorenzo's fingers tightened around her thigh. He gave his mother a look that said that was enough and changed the subject.

She tried to shake it off as the meal wore on, but couldn't. Of all the things she and Lorenzo were battling through right now, a baby was not a priority.

Unable to do justice to the delicious chicken dish Constanza had cooked because her stomach had coiled up into a tight little ball, she set down her fork. By the time the elder Riccis got up to make their departure just after ten, she was fuming. She managed a few more minutes of civility, discussing the current theater runs with Octavia while Salvatore pulled his son aside in the study.

"*Maledizione*, Lorenzo, who the hell leaked this deal?"

Lorenzo leaned against his desk and crossed his arms over his chest. He'd been hoping to avoid this discussion, had almost managed it, until his father had pulled him aside.

"I have no idea," he said flatly. "There's only been high-level people involved. But you know what it's like—when there's a juicy story waiting in the wings, someone is always willing to spill."

"And if we don't close it?" his father countered. "This is Ricci's reputation you are gambling with. It's one thing to pursue a company that wants to dance, another thing entirely to drag it kicking and screaming onto the floor."

"I will close it," Lorenzo growled. "We will dance the final waltz, Papà. But I am not a magician. I cannot summon Mark Bavaro back from South America with a snap of my fingers. You need to give me time."

"I have given you time. A year this has been dragging on, *figliolo*. This needs to be done before the next board meeting. Before they start wondering if we know what we're doing in the corner office or not."

Lorenzo scowled. "They are a bunch of overreactors with too much time on their hands."

"Who can make our lives hell if they choose to." His father crossed his arms over his chest, mirroring his pose. "I am beginning to think your ambition has got the best of you on this one."

His back stiffened. Bavaro's disappearance was raising his blood pressure. He didn't need the added pressure of his father trying to control everything around him even though he was no longer in charge of Ricci. But going head-to-head with Salvatore, he reminded himself, was like two stags locked in a fight to the finish. It never ended well.

"I am CEO of this company," he said, eyeing his father. "I will get the deal done. Back off and let me do my job."

His father gave a haughty tilt of his head. "October, Lorenzo. This needs to be signed and sealed."

Too riled up to sleep, Angie put on a swimsuit and headed for the hot tub on the terrace while her husband returned a phone call. Maybe it would unwind the Octavia-induced knots in her shoulders.

Built into the deck, with a sensational view of the Manhattan skyline, it was her favorite way to relax after a long day. She dropped her towel on the deck, set her half-finished glass of wine beside the tub and stepped into the hot, bubbling water, immersing herself up to her shoulders.

A sigh left her. Closing her eyes, she let the jets unwind the knots, ease the band of tension encircling her skull.

"In a better mood?"

Her eyes fluttered open. Her husband stood on the deck in navy trunks, a perfect male specimen in the prime of his life. Her heart rate skyrocketed as he tossed a towel over the railing. He was leaner than he'd been before, muscle and sinew arranged in a spectacular grid pattern across his pecs and abdomen. The perfect symmetry of it made her stomach curl.

She swallowed past a suddenly dry mouth. "I thought you had to make a call."

"It was a quick one." He lowered himself into the water, taking the seat opposite her. Her heartbeat calmed. His slow inventory of her, however, sent it ratcheting back up again. The bikini she had on, a halter top and briefs, wasn't overly revealing by any means, but her husband's thorough perusal made her feel as if there wasn't enough material to it. Not nearly enough.

"What happened with your father?" she blurted out, needing to distract herself from that...*heat.*

His dark gaze slid up to hers. "He is anxious about the Belmont deal. He is used to swallowing up tiny fish to build his empire. He doesn't have the patience to stalk a bigger prey, one that might not be quite so willing."

"You still haven't been able to tie down Marc Bavaro?"

"No." He exhaled a long breath and laid his head back against the tub. "He is MIA."

She studied the intensity that came off him like smoke. "What?" he asked, brow raised.

"I'm just wondering where this all-consuming drive comes from? This never-ending need for more."

He lifted a shoulder. "I was born with it. It's in my blood. Franco's, too."

"Franco has a sense of balance. A safety valve. You don't."

His gaze narrowed. "I am not my brother."

"No," she agreed. "But you weren't always like this. Franco told me that before Lucia you knew your limits. You knew how to live."

The glint in his eyes took on a dangerous edge.

"My brother likes to play amateur psychologist. My ambition is strictly my own sin, *cara*, recognized and owned."

"It's not a badge of honor," she countered. "You push yourself to unsustainable levels, Lorenzo. You are going to drive yourself into the ground someday if you don't watch it. Maybe you should take a page out of your brother's book and allow yourself to be human once in a while."

"And maybe you should tell me what happened tonight." He raised a brow. "You knew my mother was going to bring up babies. It was a foregone conclusion. Why the overreaction?"

Heat seared her belly, her concern for him dissipating on a wave of antagonism. "It was not a foregone conclusion your mother would hammer me to the wall about a subject you know I am sensitive about. Knowing that, *you* should have diverted her. *We* haven't even discussed it yet."

He inclined his head. "Perhaps I should have. But you know you and I having a baby is a reality with Franco unable to conceive."

She lifted her chin. "It's not going to happen if you keep putting this pressure on me. We've promised to try this again, Lorenzo, and I will put my heart and soul in it, as you are asking. But I need time to adjust to *us* before we think about a baby. Not to mention the fact that I need to take advantage of the career opportunities in front of me. *Now* is not a good time for a baby. You said so yourself, we have time."

"We do," he agreed. "I'm not sure I'd say we have *lots* of it because my mother is right, it could take us time to conceive. Also—" He stopped in midsentence, a wary look in his eyes.

Her stomach bottomed out. "Also *what*?"

"We miscarried last time. It could happen again. Which is why we need to give ourselves *time*."

Fear and anger balled up inside of her. "I am not ready to have this discussion."

"Because you're scared?" he countered softly. "I understand if you are, Angie. I am, too. But we have to talk about it. We can't push it away as if it doesn't exist."

She pinned her gaze on his. "I'm *saying I'm not ready*. That we need to work on *us* before we start talking babies."

"Bene." His eyes glittered in the moonlight. "I am in full agreement on that point. So why don't you come over here? You're much too far away."

Her heart slammed against her ribs. "I don't think so."

"Oh, I think so," he murmured. "The only question is if you are coming over here or I'm coming over there. You make the choice."

Her blood pulsed through her veins in a restless purr. That kiss earlier, his hands on her all evening, had stirred her senses. But she was angry, too—furious about that baby conversation and being treated like a...*vessel* for the Ricci family.

"Time's up." He pushed away from the side of the tub, snared an arm around her waist and pulled her onto his lap, wrapping her legs around his hips.

Her breath caught in her throat, heart slamming against her ribs. "What are you doing?"

"Getting to know each other again. Just like you suggested..." He shot her a look filled with sensual heat, his throaty tone arcing straight between her thighs. "Relax, *mia cara*. I intend only to kiss you. *A lot*." He lifted a brow. "What do you Americans call it? *Making out? Necking?*"

"Lorenzo," she said faintly, overwhelmed by all that heat and muscle singeing her skin, "stop playing with me."

"I don't think so," he murmured, laughter dancing in his eyes. "Isn't kissing the universal language? Maybe it will work for us, too."

She opened her mouth to tell him she was still angry with him. He lowered his head and caught her lips with his before she could get the words out. She set her palms on his shoulders to reject him, to tell him *absolutely not*. But his soft, seductive kisses seduced, persuaded. He nipped her bottom lip, sucking gently on her top one, sliding under her defenses like warm, sweet honey.

Melting from the inside out, she dug her nails into his muscular, sinewy shoulders. *Hard*.

"What?"

"I'm still mad at you. *You* can't avoid the baby issue by kissing me. I need time, Lorenzo. You have to give me that."

"Okay." He brushed his thumb over the pulse pounding at the base of her neck. "I'll give you time."

She blinked. "You will?"

"Sì."

Not expecting such an easy capitulation, she was momentarily silenced. He tucked a wisp of her hair behind her ear, dark eyes on hers. "What else is going on in that beautiful head of yours? It's like smoke coming out of your ears."

She shook her head.

"Angelina." His low, sensual tone promised retribution if she didn't spill.

"I'm scared," she said finally. "Terrified."

"Of what?"

Of letting herself want him again, *need* him again. Of letting herself feel the things she hadn't let herself feel since she'd left him because she could get hurt, because he would *see* beneath her skin as he always had. Of letting him make her whole again, then shatter her apart, because this time she wasn't sure she'd be able to pick up the pieces.

She closed her eyes. Pulled in a breath. "We were so good together. Then it all fell apart. I'm afraid of letting myself go there again only to have you shut down."

He shook his head. "I am not perfect. I have my moods, you know that. But I promise you it will not be the same. We will talk through our stumbles, work through them together. This is not about what *was*, Angelina, it is about what we are *building* together."

She swallowed past the fear bubbling up inside of her. The trust they'd built over these last emotional weeks together made her think they might be able to do it.

He tilted her chin up with his fingers. "*We* decide where this goes. But you have to commit. You have to trust. You have to believe we can do this."

"I do," she said quietly. "But we need to take it slow."

That wicked gleam in his eyes reappeared. "What do you think I'm doing?"

She didn't protest when he slid his palm to the nape of her neck and brought her back to him, his beautiful mouth claiming hers. Delivered on the leisurely, sensual make-out session he'd promised until her toes curled with pleasure. Full of heat and oh, so much promise, sweetness and play devolved into a deeper, fiery need.

She opened to his demand, his tongue stroking and licking while his hands kept her in place for his delectation. She curled her fingers in his hair, sighed his name and pulled him closer still. It had been too long, far too long since he'd touched her like this. It was like returning to heaven—a most dangerous paradise, she knew, but she couldn't deny she wanted it…wanted to revel in it.

Her husband shifted beneath her, his highly aroused body brushing against her thighs. Shock waves coursed through her nerve endings, lighting her on fire.

He lifted his mouth from hers, a wry smile curving his mouth. "This would be where the make-out session ends and something else entirely begins. Unless," he drawled, "you've changed your mind?"

Heat claimed her cheeks. All it would take was one more kiss, one sign from her she was ready and she could have him. But unleashing that kind of intimacy with her husband would bring all her walls tumbling down—it always had. And she wasn't ready for that. Not yet.

"I can wait," he murmured, tracing a knuckle down her cheek. "But be prepared, Angelina. When this does happen, one tame roll in that bed in there will not be enough."

CHAPTER EIGHT

ANGIE SPENT THE following week immersed in a flurry of activity leading up to Alexander's show. Likely a good thing given the confusing mixture of anticipation and apprehension engulfing her at the evolution of her and Lorenzo's relationship.

Their sizzling encounter in the hot tub had proven she was still as susceptible as ever to his expertly executed seductions, but had done nothing to illustrate they could make their marriage work. *That* they were going to have to prove in the days ahead.

Her husband, true to his word, was giving her the time she'd asked for. Not that he hadn't kept up a slow and steady campaign to put his hands on her whenever he could find an excuse to do so. She'd been so distracted at yesterday's rehearsal thinking about it, Alexander had had to ask her a question three times.

Determined to keep her focus, she'd buried herself in a couple of last-minute fixes to tailor her pieces for a model being substituted into the original lineup, keeping her mind firmly off her husband. Before she knew it, it was 7:00 p.m. on the night of the show, the lights had dimmed in the high-ceilinged Skylight Modern space, one of the premium, architecturally perfect Fashion Week venues, and Alexander's first model had begun her walk down the spotlit runway.

Anticipation built as one model after the next, with a few supermodels thrown in for good measure, strutted their stuff, showcasing the collection the critics said would catapult Alexander to the top of the design world this season. The buzz and applause was electric as her friend's brilliance shone, his pieces the perfect backdrop for her jewelry.

It seemed like only a few minutes had passed instead of an hour before the show was drawing to an end.

Her blood fizzled in her veins as Astrid Johansson, the world's current *it* girl, stood spotlighted at the end of the runway to wrap the show, Angie's ruby necklace glittering against her alabaster skin. A shiver chased up her spine. It was perfect, a marriage made in heaven the way the necklace framed the square neckline of the sleek, avant-garde dress.

Lorenzo leaned down from his position beside her in the front row, bringing his mouth to her ear. "The highest paid model in the world wearing your jewelry. How does it feel?"

"Amazing." And her husband looked equally stunning in a charcoal-gray Faggini suit, his swarthy coloring set off perfectly by the light blue shirt he wore beneath it. She'd seen more than one of the models eye him as they'd walked by, eating him up with their confident gazes.

Astrid made her final pass down the runway, returning hand in hand with Alexander as the music died away and the lights came up, her fellow models falling into place behind them. Cheers and applause greeted the designer, who took it all in with a big smile on his expressive face.

She was shocked when he beckoned to her, motioning for her to join him. Oh, no, she couldn't.

Lorenzo gave her a gentle shove. "*Go.* Have your moment."

She found herself moving forward on legs that felt like jelly. Taking Alexander's hand, she followed him into the spotlight. The designer turned to her, gave a little bow and clapped his hands. Her chest swelled with happiness, a hot warmth stinging the backs of her eyes as the audience applauded. Her jewelry had been her light in the darkness when everything else had been falling apart. She would never be able to express what it meant to her. She only knew in that moment, it felt as if a piece of her was sliding into place.

She gave Alexander a kiss on the cheek, stood back and returned the applause. The lights went down. Alexander pulled her backstage for interviews with the media while Lorenzo and his mother went to enjoy a cocktail. She had expected only a smattering of media would be interested in speaking to her in the shadow of Alexander's presence. She was shocked when a handful of them chose to interview her, too.

She did a couple of broadcast interviews for television, then something with a leading newspaper's style section. Surprisingly, the media's focus remained mostly on her jewelry rather than on her lineage, the critics giving her collection an enthusiastic thumbs-up.

She was pretty much floating on air by the time

Alexander hooked an arm through hers, propelled her into the crowd at the after-party and introduced her to the designers, fashion editors, models and actors starring in his next spring ad campaign, forging so many valuable connections it made her head spin.

An impenetrable glow filled her. Her career was skyrocketing, her marriage on the mend. It felt as if anything was possible.

Lorenzo watched his wife shine, her bubbly, animated demeanor taking him back to that night in Nassau when she'd transfixed him like the brightest star in the sky. The haunting, mysterious Northern Lights had had nothing on his wife that night as she'd flashed those baby blues at him, silky long lashes brushing her cheeks in a coquettish look she hadn't quite mastered, and asked him if he was going to brood all night or dance with her instead.

But even then, he realized, underneath all that sultry confidence and gutsy bravado, there had been a vulnerability to the woman in his arms, a sadness he hadn't quite been able to put a finger on—a knowledge beyond her years.

He had connected to that, even if he hadn't known it at the time. They had both been looking to escape their pain that night, he from his memories, Angelina from the inexplicably complex relationships that had formed her world. What they had found had been so powerful that for a while they had.

She caught him staring. Smiled. It was a blindingly bright smile that did something crazy to his heart. He had denied her this, the chance to be this shining light. To prove she was more than the sum of her parts. It was a mistake he refused to let haunt him.

He saw her say something to Alexander, nod at the woman they were speaking to and slip away, her long strides eating up the distance between them.

"Did your mother leave?"

"Yes." He swiped two glasses of champagne off a tray and handed her one. "She said to say thank you. To tell you your collection was impressive. And, yes," he added, a wry smile twisting his mouth, "she meant it."

Angie blinked. "Well, that's...*nice*. Did she have a good time?"

"She was in her element. Who knows," he murmured, lifting a brow, "there might be hope for the two of you yet."

"Don't get too hopeful."

He brushed a thumb across the delicate line of her jaw. "Positivity, *cara*. That's what we need here."

Her lashes lowered. "We should circulate if you don't mind."

He nodded. Kept a possessive hand at the small of her back as they made a couple of passes of the room. By the time the lights came down and the apparently wildly popular band Lorenzo had never heard of took the stage, he could feel his wife's energy level fading, her reservoir of small talk emptied out.

Tugging her into one of the intimate lounge areas, he plucked the wineglass out of her hand and pulled her onto his lap.

"Lorenzo," she murmured, "we are in public."

"At a party in full gear where no one is paying any attention to us." Setting a palm on her thigh, he pulled her closer, absorbing the tantalizing feel of her lush curves plastered against him. She looked insanely beautiful in Alexander's black dress with no back to it. Had turned every male head in the room. The need to have his hands on her was like a fire in his blood.

Bending his head, he traced the shell of her ear with his lips in a feather-light caress. His wife shivered. He moved lower, capturing her lobe between his teeth, scoring it lightly. "You are lit up tonight, *mia cara*. This is the woman I *appreciate*. The woman I was looking for."

She pulled back, eyes on his. "I needed this. For you to understand how important my work is to me."

"I do now." His voice was sandpaper-rough. "I am listening now, Angelina. Better late than never."

Needing to protect, to possess her in a way he couldn't even begin to articulate, he cupped the back of her head and kissed her. Passionate, infinite, it was a connection between them on an entirely different level than before, as if they were finally beginning to understand each other.

She slid her palm to his nape and kissed him back, the kiss turning hot and fiery. *Needy*. He moved his hand higher on her thigh, fingers tightening around the sleek, satiny skin he discovered.

A primal heat consumed him, his body pulsing to life beneath her bottom. She shifted against him, a low moan leaving her throat.

"I want inside you," he whispered. "Inside this sweet, hot body of yours. Until you feel nothing but me, *cara*."

Blood roared in Angie's head. Light exploded in her eyes. She blinked against the sudden onslaught. It took her several seconds to realize it was a photographer's flash.

Lorenzo brushed a knuckle against her cheek, a wry twist to his mouth. "That must be our cue to leave."

Her legs felt like spaghetti as he set her on her feet. He kept a firm hand on her waist as he guided her through the thick crowd, stopping to say good-night to Alexander before they exited into the cool night air.

Wrapped in a sensual haze, she curled her arms around herself as Lorenzo retrieved the car. The sports car was deposited purring at the sidewalk moments later. Lorenzo tucked her into the passenger seat, then took the wheel to drive them home.

Her pulse hummed, her blood fizzled amidst

the cacophony of sirens and honking horns that was New York, all of it blanking in her head as her senses focused on the man beside her. His quiet intensity as he controlled the powerful car and the hand he kept on her bare thigh were all she could register.

When this does happen, one tame roll in that bed will not be enough.

Her pulse jolted faster, her cheeks heated with anticipation. Her head might be wary about them, but her body was not. It wanted to experience the hunger he had promised. To feel alive again in the way only Lorenzo could make her feel.

Finally they were home. Parking the car in the garage, he helped her out, ushered her into the lift that arrived in a whir of expensive machinery. Up they went to the penthouse, where she threw her purse on a chair, legs shaking. Walking to the bank of windows that looked out on the roughly drawn skyline of Manhattan, she took a deep breath, attempted to center herself.

The soft thud of her husband's jacket hitting the chair reverberated through the room. The tread of his footsteps across the hardwood floor sent a quiver up her spine.

"You are so damn beautiful," he murmured, setting his hands on her hips. "You make my heart stop in my chest."

Her breath caught in her lungs. Frozen, paralyzed, she couldn't move, her fears, her anticipation, blanketing her in a cloud of emotion. But this wasn't about the past, she reminded herself, it was about the future. And right now, it felt like they had one. A bright, shining light she was terrified to touch.

She did it anyway. Twisting around in his arms, she took in the dark, sometimes brooding man who'd stolen her heart once and threatened to do it again. His eyes tracked her, hot and focused. Her stomach contracted. Lifting her hand, she traced the sexy stubble shadowing his jaw. It was too tempting not to touch. She pressed a kiss to the abrasive canvas, sliding over the hard line of his jaw, *knowing* him again.

He let her play, drink her fill. Then impatience won out as he slid his fingers into her hair, tilted her head back and closed his mouth over hers. Greedy, laced with sensual purpose, his carnal kiss telegraphed his intent to know all of *her* tonight. To erase the pain.

She curled her fingers into the thick muscles of his shoulders, opened to his stark demand. The slow, erotic strokes of his tongue against hers coiled the muscles in her abdomen tight, his dark, sensual taste filling her senses, seducing her with its rich male flavor.

Fingers digging into his shoulders, she hung on tight. Lorenzo slipped a hand lower to her bottom, shaping her against him. The hard thrust of his desire, a thick, pulsing heat beneath his trousers, pulled a low sound from the back of her throat. She pressed closer, drunk on the feel of him. He rocked against her, slid his steely heat against her most sensitive flesh, scoring her through the thin material of her dress. "Feel how much I want you," he murmured against her mouth. "You make me crazy, Angelina."

A shudder went through her, her knees nearly buckling beneath her. He backed her up against the windowsill, kneed her legs apart so he could stand between them. Supported by the wall, she welcomed the hot press of his flesh. Allowed him to tease her, play with her until she thought she might go up in flames.

Her hands moved to his belt, greedy, desperate

for him. Yanking the leather free of the buckle, she undid it, unbuttoned his trousers and slid down the zipper. Pushing her hands inside his pants, she cupped the thick length of him in her palms.

Lorenzo cursed low and hard. Removed her hands from him. "*Mi bellissima.* You need warming up or I will hurt you."

"No," she said, trying to free her hands. "I need you inside me."

"*Sì.*" Hard, uncompromising. He captured her hands, placed them palms-down on the sill. "Keep them there."

Eyes on hers, he sank his fingers into the knot of his tie, pulled it loose and stripped it off. Tossing it on the floor, he reached for the top buttons of his shirt and pulled them free. Her heart thrummed the frantic beat of a bird trapped in a cage as he dropped to his knees in front of her.

Reaching for her foot, he worked the delicate clasp of her shoe open, slid her foot out and tossed the stiletto aside. He did the same with the other. Setting his hands on her ankles, he trailed them up her calves to her knees. Pushed them apart with a deliberate, firm motion that had her sucking in a breath. "Lorenzo," she breathed, feeling far too exposed.

He looked up at her, an implacable expression in his dark eyes. "Stay still."

Oh, dear Lord. A shudder went through her. He pressed a kiss to the inside of both her knees, worked his way up the sensitive flesh of her inner thighs, caressing her with his mouth, the scrape of his teeth. She bit her lip, willing him on.

She was aching, pulsing for him by the time he got to where she wanted him. Ready to beg. Mouth dry, she watched as he pushed up her dress and tucked it beneath her hip, baring her lacy, black panties. A wisp of nothing—meant to seduce.

Hand on her thigh, he considered her. *Bold. Focused.* "You wore these for me?"

"Yes."

A smile tugged at his mouth. "I thought you said you weren't going to wear lingerie for me."

"I said I wouldn't greet you at the door wearing it."

A play of laughter in those dark eyes. "Appreciate the distinction."

Shifting his attention back to the job at hand,

he lowered his head and caressed her through the silk with one long stroke of his tongue. Her knees buckled. Sinking back on her palms, she braced herself against the wood. Closed her eyes as he stroked her again and again, desensitizing her, she knew, for the pleasure he would give her.

When she stopped bucking under his tongue, he pressed a kiss to her trembling abdomen, slid his fingers under the edges of the silk and stripped the panties from her. Moving back between her thighs, he spread her wide. Ran his thumb through her cleft. Blood surged from her fingertips to her toes as he examined her flesh.

"Already wet for me, *cara*." He looked up, eyes blazing. "Maybe I should stop."

She reached for him. Received a reproachful look as he put her palms back on the wood. "Move them again and I will."

She closed her eyes. Felt the heat of his breath before his tongue found the hard nub at the center of her, nudging it with sensual precision. Back and forth, up and down. When her legs started to shake, her voice a low plea, he licked her slowly, deliberately, talking to her as he did it, telling her the taste of her made him hard. Hot.

Insane for him, at the very edge, she curled her fingers into the wood. He circled her with his finger. Delved inside of her. Her muscles clenched around him, drawing him in. Slowly, relentlessly, he moved his finger in and out of her, another kind of pleasure stirring to life that was deeper. More intense.

"Look at me." His husky command brought her eyes fluttering open. Seeing him between her spread legs, pleasuring her, sent her right to the edge. "You want it like this? Or with me inside your beautiful body?"

She swallowed past the need constricting her throat, the raging hunger he inspired in her. "With you," she rasped, keeping her hands on the wood. "I want it to be with you."

Lorenzo removed his hands from his wife, swung her up in his arms and carried her into the bedroom, working to blank his mind from the emotion pouring through it. But his wife had always cast a spell over him and tonight was no exception, despite his attempts to tell himself going there was unwise.

He set her down near the bed and moved behind her to lower the zipper of her dress. Pushing it off her shoulders, Alexander's creation hit the wood floor in a swish of feather-light material.

Hands on her shoulders, he turned her around. Drank in his wife's mouthwatering curves. Lushly feminine in all the right places, her breasts were more than a handful, perfectly shaped and high, her delectable hips flaring above long, fantastic legs he wanted wrapped around him so badly, it was all he could do to keep this the leisurely seduction he'd planned.

Stripping off his shirt and pants, his gaze never left her. Kicking his clothes aside, he snaked an arm around her waist, pulled her to him and plastered her curves against the length of his body. Fingers curving around her jaw, he dropped a lingering kiss on her mouth. Shared with her the essence of their mutual passion until the raw, unvarnished truth of their connection swelled him so hard he thought he might break in two.

This time when she reached for him, her touch like silk around his throbbing length, he arched into it, desperate for more.

"That's it." His breath was hot against her ear.

"I've missed your hands on me, *mia cara*. I *crave* them."

His skin began to burn, *tremble*, her exploration of his body firing his blood. He closed his eyes, primal sounds leaving the back of his throat as she stroked him to the edge.

When he could take it no longer, he pushed her hands away, sank his palms into her hips and lifted her onto the bed. The moonlight spilling in the French doors edged across her face, illuminating the beautiful vulnerability he was starting to believe was the truth of her.

He slid his hands around her back, released the catch of her bra and threw it to the floor. Her full, swollen breasts were a temptation he couldn't resist. A shudder raked through her as he swept his thumbs across the tips.

"Like ripe, delectable fruit," he murmured, lowering his head to her. He took a nipple in his mouth and sucked hard. She gasped, threw back her head and pushed her flesh farther into his mouth. He devoured her, satisfied his hunger. Played her other nipple between his thumb and forefinger while he brought the hard bud to a swollen erectness with his lips and teeth.

She moaned as he lavished the same attention on her other breast, digging her fingers in his hair. *"Please."*

Her broken plea contracted his insides. He joined her on the bed, shackled his fingers around her ankles and bent them back so she was open to him. Moving between her thighs, he palmed his length, brought himself to her slick entrance and rocked against her so just the tip pushed inside.

"You want me, *cara*?"

She nodded, her big blue eyes glued to his.

"Tell me how much."

"All of you," she gasped. "I want all of you."

Bracing a palm on the bed, he tipped his hips forward and filled her with another inch. "Lorenzo," she breathed, arching up to meet him, "I need you."

A primal satisfaction claimed him. All of those nights since she'd left when no one else would do, when her memory had made a mockery of his libido, were vindicated as she lay begging beneath him, beautiful and oh, so vulnerable. Exactly as he'd wanted her. And yet, as he rocked forward again, her body clenching around him like a hot, silken glove, he would have been delusional to deny he was as affected as she was.

He leaned forward, slicking his tongue across her bottom lip in an erotic caress that made her clench tighter around him. "There is no going back," he rasped, "only forward. Tell me you understand that."

"Yes." She arched her hips, eyes glazed. *"More."*

He buried himself inside her with a smooth, powerful stroke. Her gaze met his in an electric, soul-destroying connection. "You feel like heaven, *cara*. Perfection."

Her slick, aroused body absorbed him, stretched to accommodate his length and girth. He gritted his teeth, forced himself to hang on. Fine tremors snaked through her body, her inner muscles rippling around him. He moved inside her then with hard, powerful drives designed to drive her to orgasm. He lacked his usual finesse, but was beyond caring. Her fingers clutched his hips as his big body rode hers, claimed her, found that spot deep inside her that made her moan with pleasure.

She arched into it, wanting everything he had to give. He braced himself on one arm, slipped the other hand between her legs and found the bundle of nerves at her center. "I can feel you clenching around me," he murmured, stroking his thumb teasingly over her clitoris. "Like that," he whispered when she jerked beneath his touch. "And that," he said as another shiver raked through her. "Come for me, *cara*."

His next firm caress set her off. Her husky groan, the way she gloved him in a tight squeeze, pushed him into a violent, body-shaking release. Relinquishing control, he tightened his fingers around her hips, drove into her and made her come apart a second time.

Lorenzo was awake long after his wife fell asleep in his arms. Soft and warm, her body curved against his, their fit together was so perfect it was as if she'd been made to fill in his missing spaces. To complete the parts of him that had been empty so long he'd had no idea they still existed.

A knot fisting his stomach, he disentangled himself from his wife and lay staring at the sky through the window overhead. He'd crossed a line tonight—allowing this thing between him and Angelina to become emotional when he'd promised himself he wouldn't. It had been that kind of a night, to be sure, but he knew if he wasn't careful, he'd start walking down a path he could never go and it would be Angelina who got hurt, not him.

He'd been falling in love with his wife when she'd left, his instincts warning him if he let himself, he would have fallen harder for Angelina than he had ever fallen for Lucia. His love for Lucia had been a pure, untainted first love that lacked the passion and emotion he and Angelina had shared. The depth of his feelings for Angelina, the betrayal those feelings had seemed to Lucia, the youth and unhappiness Angelina had displayed that had made her an unsure bet, had made him cauterize his feelings, refuse to acknowledge them.

And his instincts had been dead-on, he thought, staring up at the cloudy night sky. Angelina had walked out as soon as the going had gotten tough, had made a mockery of the vows they'd made. And that was why certain lines could never be crossed.

If he was smart, he would follow his original

plan. Burn out the attraction between him and his wife until it no longer held any power over him.

Now that he had her back in his bed, he intended to do exactly that.

CHAPTER NINE

"How about you come to Mallorca in a couple of weeks? I have to be at our flagship property for a few days. You can meet with the management team and we can go through the last few points face-to-face."

Lorenzo blew out a breath. He'd spent two weeks anticipating Marc Bavaro's return from South America and now he wanted him to gallivant off to *Spain*, Belmont's global headquarters, to make this deal happen? He ran a global corporation, for God's sake, three times the size of Bavaro's. How the hell did he have time for that?

"As much as I'd love to," he said in an even tone, "my schedule is insane. We can't do it before then?"

"I'm headed to London as we speak. I'm not back to New York until mid-October."

Too late, with the board meeting looming. "I'll

see what I can do," Lorenzo conceded. "How long are you thinking?"

"Come for a couple of days. We can have dinner with my brother, Diego, the night you arrive, then we'll do the management meeting the next morning. Oh—" the CEO's voice dropped to an intimate purr "—and bring your beautiful wife... she can keep Penny company."

He wasn't sure Bavaro lusting after Angelina was going to go over so well in his current mood. "Angie is in her busy period. I'll have to check her schedule."

"Let me know." The roar of a jet engine fired in the background. "I should go."

He cut off the call. Turned the air blue. Gillian popped her head in his office and asked if he needed help. He told her to clear his schedule for the time in Mallorca, then turned his thoughts to his wife. How to get her to agree to go to Spain was the challenge. She was so busy with commissions after Faggini's show she'd even hired a couple of part-time designers to help with the rush. She would balk at a trip, no doubt about it.

He sat back in his chair and contemplated a solution. Things had been better than good between them. They were learning to compromise, to manage their expectations of each other. They were communicating both in bed and out of it. His marriage was *working*. The last thing he needed was to rock the boat.

But this, he thought, tapping his fingers on the desk, was necessary.

A plan came to him. It was a good one. Satisfied, he picked up the phone.

"I have a proposal for you."

Angelina cradled her mobile against her ear as she put down her pliers, the intimate, seductive edge to her husband's voice unleashing a wave of heat beneath her skin. The huskiness, she knew, came from the inhuman working hours he was keeping.

"If it involves sleep for you, I'm all for it," she said lightly. "What time were you up this morning?"

"Five. And, yes, it involves sleep for both of us," he replied in a throaty tone that sent goose bumps to her heated skin. "Well," he amended, "it involves a bed and *us*. Sleep not so much."

Her heart beat a jagged rhythm. They hadn't

been able to get enough of each other since Alexander's party, thus contributing to *her* sleeping deficit. Not that she was complaining. She was so happy she was afraid to blink, because history had taught her something *would* implode in her face if she did.

But she wasn't *thinking* that way, she reminded herself. "What are you proposing?"

"The only way I can pin Marc Bavaro down is to hook up with him at his property in Mallorca in a couple of weeks' time. Penny's going. He wants you to come, too."

She pressed a palm to her temple. "Lorenzo... I have so much work to do before Christmas."

"That's part of my proposal. You come with me to Spain and I will absolve you of any social obligations until the hotel opening in October."

"What are you going to do? Go to them alone?"

"*Sì.*"

She didn't like the idea of her gorgeous husband attending all those events alone the way women fell all over him. Leaving the country for a week was also an unwise idea given the work in front of her.

But how could she say no after everything Lorenzo had done for her? He had been her rock as she'd navigated her emotional visits with her mother, pushed her to hire a couple of assistants to keep her sanity with all the work pouring in. And when she was exhausted from managing them, he deposited her bodily into bed when she no longer recognized her limits. She wasn't sure what she would have done without him.

"I will take you to Portofino for a couple of days afterward." Her husband's voice lowered to a sexy rasp. "We can do walks through the village. I'll take you to that seafood restaurant you love…"

Her heart turned over. By far her most magical memories with Lorenzo were from that heavenly week they'd spent together in the tiny fishing village on the Italian Riviera on their honeymoon, the view from the Riccis' villa perched in the hills spectacularly romantic. It had been impossibly perfect with their strolls through the cobblestone streets, leisurely, seaside dinners and long, uninhibited nights of lovemaking in which her husband had taught her wicked things, *delicious* things her innocent mind could only have dreamed of.

Going back would be like walking into a piece

of the past she wasn't sure she was ready for, but perhaps that was exactly what she needed to do.

"Well?" her husband prompted. "Say yes. It will be good for us, *cara*."

She blew out a breath. "Okay. But I can't be gone longer than a week. And I'm holding you to your promise."

"Bene." Satisfaction laced his tone. "I'll get Gillian to work with you on the details. *Grazie mille, bella.* I should go."

She hung up. Stared at all the pieces on her desk that needed to be finished. Thought of the massive influx of orders to be filled. She was a tiny operation—she wasn't built for this.

Panic clawed at her insides. She couldn't afford to mess up this chance she'd been given. The interest in her work following Alexander's show was a once-in-a-lifetime opportunity to make her name. But neither was she prepared to mess up her marriage.

She could do this. She just needed to lean on the designers she'd hired and make a plan.

Angie worked like a demon over the next two weeks, making a good dent in the list of commissions. Reserving the trickier pieces for when she got back, she handed the rest of the work over to her assistants and stepped on the jet for the trip to Mallorca with Lorenzo.

Shocked at how exhausted she was, she put the reclining seat back as soon as dinner had been served and slept while her machine of a husband worked.

When she woke, it was to the darkest of ebony eyes and a very seductive kiss from her husband. "Wake up, sleeping beauty. We're about to land."

She blinked. "We *aren't.*"

"We are. A half hour tops. Go freshen up so you can have some breakfast before we land."

She slid out of her seat and headed for the bedroom, where she changed her top, so she wouldn't look so wrinkled when they met the driver, and freshened her hair and makeup. Breakfast, however, wasn't to be. Her stomach still felt like it was 2:00 a.m. Coffee and orange juice would have to suffice.

The driver took them up into the lush green mountains of Mallorca's peaceful northwest coast to the Belmont Mallorca, considered to be one of the world's finest hotels. Nestled into a valley surrounded by soaring peaks, its two stone manor houses offered a spectacular view of a medieval village.

Still inordinately tired, she took a nap in the afternoon in their beautiful airy suite to arm her for a late dinner while Lorenzo spent the afternoon with Marc. But even after she woke and pulled herself out of the white-silk-draped canopy bed and showered, her limbs still felt as if they were weighted with lead.

She hadn't felt this inexplicably tired since the first trimester of her pregnancy, she mused as she stood at the wardrobe selecting a dress to wear for dinner. Ice slid through her veins… *No. There was no way.* She couldn't be. She was on the pill. She had been so careful.

Rationality, however, did not stop her from flying into the bedroom to find her purse, where she retrieved her birth control pills and found they were all accounted for. Slackening with relief, she saw the antibiotics she'd been taking following a dental procedure. Remembering she hadn't taken one today, she popped one into her mouth, swallowed it with a gulp of water, then padded back to the wardrobe to choose her dress.

A cream-colored jersey sheath called to her. She pulled it off the hanger, then froze, her stomach bottoming out. *Antibiotics and birth control pills*... Hadn't she heard somewhere...

Lorenzo watched Angelina in the mirror as he did up his shirt. Stunning in a knee-length ivory dress with a floral scarf draped around her neck, she was amazing to look at as always, but it was the preoccupied air about her that held his attention. He hadn't seen it in weeks.

"You okay?"

She nodded. "Just tired. Sorry, I'm quiet I know."

He did up the last button of his shirt and tucked it into his pants. "You don't ever have to be sorry about being quiet. I just want to make sure you're okay."

"I'm fine." She turned back to the mirror and spritzed some perfume behind her ears.

"Is it work?"

She shook her head. "It's fine. I'll catch up when I get back."

"Then what is it?"

She spun around, a frown creasing her brow.

"You don't have to treat me with kid gloves, Lorenzo. I'm *fine*."

He lifted a brow. She expelled a breath. "I am a little stressed about work. And the time change kills me."

He crossed over to her. "Try and put it out of your head and enjoy the week," he murmured, tracing a thumb over her cheek. "It's only a few days. You deserve a break."

She nodded.

"There is no goal tonight, *amore mio*. Unless you count paying attention to me," he added huskily, thumb sweeping over the lush fullness of her lips. "That is most definitely on the agenda."

Color stained her cheeks. He lowered his head and pressed his lips to her temple, breathing in the sexy, Oriental fragrance of her, her perfume the perfect match for his strong, sensual wife. They were intoxicating, both the scent and her.

For a moment, he just held her, drank her in. Knew, in that moment, he felt more for her than he would ever admit. More than he should.

Her head dropped against his chest. "We should go," she said quietly, but she didn't move.

His mouth curved. Sliding his fingers through hers, he moved his lips to her ear. "Hold that thought."

Dinner with the Bavaro brothers took place in the Belmont's famed terrace restaurant, with its spectacular view of the mountains, the live piano music lending a distinctly sophisticated atmosphere to the setting. Marc's brother, Diego, the Belmont's other controlling shareholder, joined them for dinner along with his wife, Ariana. With Penny to round out the table of six, it was an entertaining and lively dinner.

Diego, who had been a bit of a dark horse during the negotiations, content to let Marc take the lead, could have been a double for his brother with his swarthy, dark Mediterranean looks and lean build. But that was where the similarities ended. Whereas Marc was cagey, careful in what he revealed, Diego was an extrovert who liked to hear the sound of his own voice.

If Lorenzo got the younger Bavaro brother talking, he might make some progress. He waited until the fine Spanish wine had had a chance to mellow all of them, and an amiable, content atmosphere settled over the table. Sitting back in his chair, wineglass balanced on his thigh, he eyed Diego.

"I'm sensing some hesitation on your part. If the regulatory issues aren't going to be a problem in most jurisdictions, perhaps you can tell me where the pause is coming from?"

Diego took a sip of his wine and set down the glass. "My father is concerned the Belmont legacy will cease to exist with the sale. That you will absorb what you desire of our marquee locations to fill the empty dots on the map, then dispose of the rest."

A warning pulse rocketed through him. That was exactly what he intended to do—certainly the Bavaros had been smart enough to figure that out?

"We'll have to see what our assessment says," he said coolly. "But since I am offering to pay you a fortune for this chain, more than half again what it's worth, I would think it would keep you from lying awake at night worrying about it."

"It's not always about money," Diego responded. "It's about family pride. National pride. Spaniards look up to Belmont as a symbol of international success. It is bad enough to have it eaten up by a foreign entity, but to have its name extinguished along with it? It negates a hundred-year-old legend."

"It's always about the money," Lorenzo rejected. "Nothing lasts forever. You wait a few more years and you'll get half what I'm offering."

"Perhaps." Diego lifted a shoulder. "You want to make my father happy? Put a clause in the deal that you will keep the name."

Heat surged through him. He kept the fury off his face. *Just.* "What sense would that make?" he countered. "This deal will make Ricci the number one luxury hotel chain in the world. To split the brands would be counterproductive."

Silence fell over the table. Lorenzo eyed the younger Bavaro brother. "May I ask why this is coming up at the eleventh hour?"

"My father's feelings have grown stronger on the issue." Diego pursed his lips. "I'm not saying it's a deal breaker. I'm saying it's a major twist in the road."

Lorenzo's brain buzzed. His own father would do the same, he knew—would refuse to see his legacy destroyed. He couldn't necessarily blame the Bavaros. What infuriated him was that this hadn't come up earlier. It changed the entire land-scape of the deal.

"This acquisition needs to happen," Lorenzo said evenly. "If this is the issue, you need to get your father onside. There will be no postsale con-ditions attached to it. It is what it is."

Diego's eyes flashed. "It was never our inten-tion to sell, as you know."

That was when Lorenzo knew he had a big, big problem on his hands.

Angie paced the suite while she waited for her husband, who was having an after-dinner cognac with the Bavaro brothers. After the tension-filled end to the meal, she was glad to have escaped, but now she had a much bigger issue on her hands than her combustible spouse.

Penny had driven her to the local pharmacy on the pretext of finding some allergy pills. She'd shoved two pregnancy tests on the counter in-stead, two *positive* pregnancy tests that now lay in the bathroom garbage can, irrefutable evidence that fate had once again taken a hold of her life in the most indelible way.

How could this possibly have happened? What were the odds? What was she going to do?

Unable to breathe, she crossed to the windows and stood looking out at the dark mass of the mountains. She knew this baby was a gift. Even as sure as she'd been at twenty-two she hadn't been ready to have a child, as terrified as she'd been she wouldn't be a good mother given her own history, she'd developed a bond with her unborn child, a wonder at the life she and Lorenzo had created together.

She felt the same way now. But she was also scared. *Terrified.* The timing was all wrong. There was no way she could run her business, be a mother and juggle her and Lorenzo's busy social schedule all at the same time. And then there was the thought of losing another baby that sent panic skittering through her bones.

It was too soon. *Too much.*

Anxiety clawed at her throat, wanting, needing to escape. The click of the suite door brought her spinning around. The look on her husband's face kept all the anxiety buried inside.

"What happened?"

He walked to the bar, threw ice in a glass and

poured himself a drink. "Preserving the Belmont name is going to be an issue."

"You don't think they'll give on it?"

He took a long gulp of the Scotch. Leaned back against the bar. "I don't know."

"Maybe you need to talk to the father? He seems to be the roadblock."

"I'd have to go over Marc and Diego's heads. It would be a last resort."

She frowned. "They didn't mention *any* of this before? Surely they knew it might be an issue?"

"I'm fairly sure I would remember if they had."

The biting sarcasm in his voice straightened her spine. She absorbed the incendiary glow in his eyes, the flammable edge to him she remembered so well from the past. *This* was the old Lorenzo—the one who could transform into a remote stranger in the blink of an eye, focused only on the end goal and to hell with anyone in his path.

Tension knotted her insides, the need to know this wasn't devolving into the old them burning a hole in her insides. Not now, not with the news she was holding inside.

She wrapped her arms around herself, fingernails digging into the soft flesh of her upper arms.

"It was a rhetorical question," she said quietly. "I know this deal is important to you, Lorenzo, but it either works or it doesn't. You need to be able to find a way to walk away from these things and not let them get to you like this. *Consume* you."

He gave her a scathing look. "It's a fifteen-billion-dollar deal, Angelina. Ricci's reputation rides on it."

"And yours," she said quietly. "Isn't that the real issue here? You losing face? You becoming anything less than the unbeatable Lorenzo Ricci, king of the blockbuster deal?"

"This is not about me," he growled, voice sharp as a blade. "It's about my family's reputation. Rumors about the deal are running rampant…investors are getting antsy. It is my responsibility to close this acquisition."

"And if you don't?" She shook her head. "One of these days you *will* lose. You are only human. Then what? Would it be the end of the world? You have fifty of these deals you *have* landed, Lorenzo. Isn't that enough to command the confidence of your investors?"

His jaw turned to stone. "You have no idea what you're talking about."

"Maybe not," she agreed. "But I do know how I feel. You like this—I've seen it before. *This* always marks the beginning of one of your binges— it scares me where it will end."

"I'm good," he said harshly. "*We* are good. Stop trying to make problems where there aren't any."

Was she? The jet lag was killing her, her head too achy and full, her emotions all over the place. But now was not the time to tell Lorenzo about their baby. To make him understand why getting this right was so important to her.

"You wanted us to be an open book," she said, lifting her gaze to his. "Here I am, telling you how I feel."

He prowled over to her and pressed a hard kiss to her lips. "And I'm telling you, you don't need to worry. We are fine. I just need a few minutes to take the edge off."

She sank her teeth into her lower lip. Nodded. He ran a finger down her cheek, his eyes softening. "You're exhausted. You need rest. Go to bed. I'll join you in a few minutes."

"You should come, too. You didn't sleep at all last night."

He nodded, but it was an absentminded nod

that told her he wouldn't be coming for a while. She went to bed, but it was hard to sleep, empty in the beautiful bed without him, the intimacy that had wrapped itself around them the past few weeks missing, leaving her chilled and scared to the bone about what lay ahead.

Lorenzo went to bed at two. Extinguishing the lights, he slid into bed with his sleeping wife, no closer to a solution to his problem than he had been two hours before. The urge to wake his wife, to bury his agitation in her beautiful, irresistible body, was a powerful force. But she was so peaceful, so deeply asleep, he couldn't do it.

He thought about how quiet she'd been earlier, his instincts telling him something was still off. He was so scared of missing something again, of not *seeing* what he should see.

Inhaling her scent, he slipped an arm around her waist and pulled her against him, her back nestled to his chest. She murmured something in her sleep and cuddled closer.

A smile on his lips, he pressed his mouth to the sweet curve of her neck. To the silky soft skin of her cheek. The salt that flavored his lips caught him off guard. Levering himself up on his elbow, he studied her beautiful face in the moonlight. She had been crying.

His fingers curled, the urge to shake her awake and make her tell him what was wrong a furious current that sizzled his blood. They had promised to be open books with each other and still she was keeping things from him.

He forced himself to resist waking her, drawing her back against his side. Tomorrow in Portofino would be soon enough to discover what was eating his wife.

CHAPTER TEN

PORTOFINO WAS AS lovely and picturesque as Angie remembered, with its narrow, cobblestone streets, pastel-hued houses dotting the Italian Riviera and bustling shops, restaurants and luxury hotels lining its half-moon-shaped harbor.

Lorenzo had taken her to their favorite seaside restaurant following his meetings in Mallorca and their short plane ride over from Spain. He had come down from his volatile mood of the night before, his attention focused solely on her. Too much so, she thought nervously, fidgeting with her water glass as he slid her another of those long looks he'd been giving her. The secret she carried was burning a hole inside of her.

She had been waiting for the right time to tell him her news, but it just hadn't seemed to come. Lorenzo had been working the entire plane ride and something about "Could you pass me the tartar sauce, and, oh, by the way, I'm pregnant" wasn't working for her.

Her stomach did a slow curl. So here she was, making every attempt to look like she was enjoying herself and hoping her husband bought the performance.

Lorenzo snapped the spirit menu closed and handed it to the hovering waiter. "I think we'll take the check," he said in Italian.

Angie's heart skipped a beat. "I thought you said you wanted a brandy."

"I'll make an espresso at home."

The deliberate look on his face made her heart beat faster. She had the feeling he hadn't bought her act for a minute. Blood throbbed at her temples as he settled the bill, wrapped his fingers firmly around hers and they walked up the hill toward the villa.

Embraced by fuchsia-and-coral-colored bougainvillea that climbed its whitewashed walls, Octavia's retreat from her busy city life was paradise personified. Although, Angelina allowed, as Lorenzo slid the key in the door and ushered her in, her mother-in-law's description of it as her "simple abode" hardly seemed apt. The dark-wood, sleek little villa with its cheery, colorful accents that matched its vibrant surroundings, was hardly *simple*.

She walked out onto the terrace while her husband made an espresso. Hands resting on the railing, she drank in the spectacular view as a breeze lifted her hair in a gentle caress. *Paradise.* If only she could just get the damn words out.

Lorenzo returned, settled himself into one of the comfortable chairs arranged for an optimum view of the sea and deposited the coffee cup in his hand on the table. Her heart lurched in her chest at the stare he leveled at her. "You going to tell me what's wrong?"

His neutral tone did nothing to lessen the intensity of his expression. Heat stained her cheeks.

"Lorenzo—"

"*Dannazione*, Angelina." His fury broke through his icy control. "How many times do we have to have this discussion? I can't help you, *we* can't do this, unless you talk to me. I have spent the entire dinner waiting for you to tell me whatever it is that's eating you. Do you think I can't read you well enough to know that something is?"

Her tongue cleaved to the roof of her mouth.

"You weren't in the right state of mind last night and it wasn't a discussion for a restaurant."

"How about before dinner in the very *private* suite at the Belmont?" Fire flared in his eyes. "I asked you if something was wrong. You said no. Then I come to bed only to discover you've been crying."

She blinked. "How do you know?"

"I checked on you when I came to bed. You had tearstains on your face."

Oh. She wrapped her arms around herself. Took a deep breath. "I couldn't understand why I was so tired yesterday. Jet lag always gets me, yes, but I hadn't felt like that since my pregnancy. I went to check I'd taken my pills after my nap and found the antibiotics I've been on in my purse. It made me put two and two together."

His face went utterly still. "To equal what?"

"Antibiotics can interfere with birth control," she said quietly. "I'm pregnant, Lorenzo."

A behavioral psychologist could have scoured his face and found nothing it was so blank. It was in his eyes that she saw his reaction—deep, dark, raw emotion that made the knots inside her tie themselves tighter.

"How do you know?"

"Penny drove me to the pharmacy."

He was silent for so long she couldn't stand it. "What are you thinking?"

"I'm trying to absorb it," he said huskily. "In my mind, we were waiting."

Not so much.

"You're scared?"

She nodded. Her chin wobbled, the emotion welling up inside of her threatening to bubble over. "I know I should recognize this as a wonderful thing and I do, but all I can feel is the fear right now. I *hate* that I feel that way, but I do."

His gaze softened. "Come here."

She moved to him on unsteady legs. He pulled her onto his lap, wrapping his arms around her. "You're allowed to be scared," he murmured against her hair. "We lost our baby. It was scary, it was unexpected. It wasn't supposed to happen."

She closed her eyes and burrowed into his warmth. Waking up to those severe abdominal cramps, the spotting, *knowing* something was wrong had been so scary. The loss of something so special like losing a piece of herself. But it was the fear she had somehow precipitated it that haunted her the most. Her mixed emotions, her worry she wasn't ready to be a mother, that she wouldn't be a *good* mother. It was a fear she'd never shared with Lorenzo because she had been too ashamed to even think it, let alone *admit* it to him.

She curled her fingers around a handful of his T-shirt, tugged at the soft material. "I worry about what this is going to do to *us*. We're in a good place right now. What's going to happen when the stress of this kicks in?"

"We're going to manage it," he said quietly. "Just like we've managed everything else. Life isn't going to stop throwing curveballs at us, Angelina. That's the way it works."

"I know." She bit her lip. "But what about my career? I have worked so hard for what I've achieved. I can barely keep up with the demand as it is. How am I going to handle it with a child?"

"Keep your assistants on a full-time basis. Do what you need to do. We're lucky money is no object for us."

"And if I want to get a nanny?"

His face stilled. "We can talk about it."

She read his reluctant expression. "You want me home raising our child just like your mother was."

"I know I need to make concessions," he conceded stiffly. "I'm just not sure I want a nanny bringing up our child." He lifted his hand in a typically Italian gesture. "A child needs its mother. You, of all people, should know that."

She wasn't sure what sparked the violent reaction that rose up inside of her—fire licking her spine, heat flaming her cheeks. Whether it was because this was Lorenzo and his perfect family he was using as a benchmark, or whether he saw her as a deficient product of her mother's lack of maternal ability and wanted to make sure his child had better.

She pushed a hand against his chest, rolled to her feet in a jerky movement and stood facing him, hands planted on her hips.

"Angelina—"

"No, you're right." Fury crackled beneath every syllable. "I do know what it's like. I also know what it's like to feel as if my life is utterly out of control—to navigate those curveballs you talked about on a daily basis, to not know what's going to blow up in my face next. I am an *expert* at navigating the perils of childhood, Lorenzo. So trust me when I say, I will never neglect our child."

His jaw hardened. "I didn't say that."

"Yes, you did." She lifted her chin. "A part-time nanny would not be detrimental to our child's development."

"You didn't say part-time, you said 'a nanny.'"

"Well, I'm saying it now. I *will* be in control of this, too, Lorenzo. You will not decide how this works and negate all my decisions or I will take the Ricci heir and walk so fast you won't know what hit you."

His gaze narrowed, an icy black flame burning to life. "You need to settle down and not say things you'll regret, *cara*. You are overreacting."

"Overreacting? You are the one who *blackmailed* me back into this marriage."

"*Sì.*" A flash of white teeth in his arrogant face. "A marriage you promised to make work. And just to point out—*you* have sprung this on me just this minute. *I* have not had the time to process the fact that I am going to be a father. You might give me some time to do that."

Guilt lanced through her. She thought she *might* be overreacting as she stood there, chest heaving with God knew what emotions, but it was all just too...*much.*

Lorenzo snagged an arm around her waist and pulled her back down on his lap.

"We," he said, visibly pulling himself back under control, "are going to figure this out. *You* are not going to create one of your dramas to throw us off track. There will be no decrees from me, Angelina, but we *will* talk this out in whatever way we need to to reach common ground."

She stared at him for a long moment. Took a deep breath and nodded.

"That said," he continued, "what was it about what I just said that set you off?"

She was silent for a moment. "Part of it is Octavia. How you build her up to be this mythical creature who can do no wrong—the earth mother who created the perfect family. The other part of it is about me, I think. I worry about being a good mother. I worry I don't have the skills to do it— that it isn't in my DNA."

His gaze softened. "You have a deep, loving relationship with your sister. You have mothered your own mother since you were fifteen. How is that not a sign you will be a caring mother?"

The adrenaline surging through her veins eased, her breath escaping in a slow exhale. She'd never thought of it that way. She'd thought she'd had no choice but to take care of her mother because that's what family did. But in reality, she could have done the opposite as James had—as her father had—and pretended the problem didn't exist, that the disease ravaging her mother wasn't tearing her apart. But *that* hadn't been in her DNA.

Her tendency to sabotage the good before it disappeared was suddenly cast in a bright, blinking light. "I'm sorry," she said quietly. "It's my instinct to reach for anger, to lash out when I don't know how I feel…when my emotions confuse me."

"I know you now." His stare was level, unwavering. "I'm not going to let you drive wedges between us because of your fears. This baby is our second chance to do this right, Angelina. But you have to fight for us like I'm fighting for us. Fight for what we are building here."

She nodded. Rested her forehead against his. "I know. I'm sorry. Old habits die hard."

He lifted a hand to cup her jaw. Brought his mouth to hers. She met his kiss hungrily, wanting, *needing* him to wipe away her fears. Because she knew in her heart they could do this—that what they were building was more powerful, more *real* than what they'd been before. She just needed to get past the fear.

He slid a hand into her hair, held her more securely while he consumed her, *feasted* on her. She kissed him back, giving of herself without reservation. Hotter, brighter, the flame between them burned until it was an all-consuming force that engulfed them both.

Undoing the buttons that ran up the front of her dress, he exposed her body to his gaze. She shivered as he took the weight of her in his palms and teased her nipples into hard, aching points with his tongue, his teeth, nipping then laving her with soothing caresses. Moaned when he drew her deeper into the heat of his mouth, his hot, urgent caress turning her core liquid.

His eyes were hungry when he broke the contact, devouring her face with an intensity she felt to her toes. "My child will suckle at your breast," he rasped. "Do you know what that does to me? How much that makes me want you? How can this not be right, Angelina?"

Her heart slammed hard against her breastbone, stealing her breath. Her gaze locked with his for a long, suspended moment before he lowered his head and covered her mouth with his. Sliding his hand up the inside of her thigh, he found the strip of silk that covered her most intimate flesh.

She spread her thighs wider, giving him better access. Sweeping aside the silk, he dipped inside her heat, stroking her with a touch that made her arch her back, mewl a low sound of pleasure at the back of her throat.

Nothing, no feeling on this earth compared to being in Lorenzo's arms. He had become her addiction again as surely as she'd known he would. And yet it was more, so much more this time.

He sank two fingers inside of her. She gasped, her body absorbing the intrusion. He worked them in and out, his urgent, insistent rhythm sweeping her along with it until she was clenching around him. Begging him to let her come.

He pressed a kiss to her temple. "We should go inside."

"Here," she insisted, desperate to have him.

She slid off him, moved her hands under her dress and shimmied her lacy underwear off.

Straddling him, she left enough room between them to find the button of his trousers and release it. He gritted his teeth as she slid the zipper past his throbbing flesh, closed her hands around him.

"Angie," he groaned, eyes blazing. "The neighbors could see us."

She ignored him, stroking her hands over him, luxuriating in the velvet-over-steel texture of him. He was made to give pleasure to a woman and she wanted him to lose control as surely as she did each and every time he drove her to it.

Her husband closed his eyes. Let go. Told her how much he loved it, how good it felt, how much it turned him on to have her hands on him. Her blood burned hotter, so hot she thought she might incinerate.

He let her have her fill, then he took control, snagging an arm around her waist and pulling her forward. Lifting her with one hand anchored around her hips, he palmed himself, brought his flesh to her center and dipped into her slick, wet heat.

His penetration was controlled and so slow it almost killed her. She shuddered, clenching her fingers around his nape. The look of pleasure written across his beautiful face, the naked play of emotion he couldn't hide were all she needed to fall tumbling into him. And this time she did it with all of her.

She caught his mouth with hers. "More."

He gripped her hips tighter and impaled her in one impatient movement that made her gasp. Clutching his shoulders, she absorbed the power of him. How he filled her in ways she'd never been filled before. How what they were becoming accessed even deeper pieces of her than she'd even knew existed.

She knew in that moment she'd never stopped loving him. Wondered how she ever could have denied it. The admission sent a frisson of wild, unadulterated fear up her spine.

Eyes on his, she rode it out, anchored herself to him with the contact, trusted him with all of her. Circling her hips, she took him deep. He was hard as a rock and thick enough to stretch her muscles to the very edge of her pleasure. She sucked in a breath as the power of him caressed her with every hard stroke, pushing her toward a release she knew would be intense and earth-shattering.

The glazed look in his eyes told her he was just

as far gone as she was. Banding his arm tighter around her hips, he drove deeper, harder.

"Lorenzo—" His name was a sharp cry on her lips.

He shifted his hand to the small of her back, urging her to lean forward, to grind against him, to take her pleasure. She moaned low in her throat as his body set her on fire. He drove up into her shaking body until he hit that place that gave her the sweetest pleasure. Nudged it again and again until she splintered apart in a white-hot burst of sensation that knocked her senseless.

Her husband joined her on a low, husky groan, his big body shaking with the force of his release. It was erotic and soul-searing in a way that sucked the breath from her lungs.

She wasn't sure how long they stayed like that, joined with each other, before Lorenzo picked her up and carried her to bed. The dusky shadows of the room enveloped her as sleep carried her off to unconsciousness, her limbs entangled with his.

He had to move faster.

Lorenzo pressed his finger against the biometric scanner, heart pounding in his chest. The lights of the sports car, still running in the street, illuminated the number 29 on the red door.

The system flashed green. Jamming his hand on the handle, he swung open the door and strode inside, scanning the dimly lit main floor. Nothing.

Lucia had called from his study.

Running for the stairs, he climbed to the second level. Deep voices echoed above. The intruders were still there...

Back against the wall, he scaled the length of the narrow hallway until he reached the pool of light sprawling from his study. Silence, black silence, pumped ice through his veins.

He pushed the half-ajar door open. Levering himself away from the wall, he slipped inside. Stopped in his tracks. Blood—red, sharp, metallic, everywhere. His heart came to a shuddering halt. He followed the trail that dripped slowly to the mahogany floor up to the woman at the center of it all, slumped over his desk.

The world began to spin. Snapping out of the trance he was in, he started toward her—to help her, save her. A flash of movement—fingers banded around his arm. He lifted his other arm

*to strike. The glimmer of the officer's gold badge
froze his hand in midair.*

He was too late. He was always too late...

Lorenzo sat bolt upright in bed, sweat whipping from his face. His heart, gripped by terror
and grief, stalled in his chest. It took him a full
two or three seconds to realize the woman beside
him was not Lucia, it was Angelina.

He was in bed with Angelina in Portofino.

She stirred now, putting out a hand to touch
him. He set a palm to her back and told her to
go to sleep. Making a sound in the back of her
throat, she curled an arm around her pillow and
went back to sleep.

He sucked in deep breaths, attempted to regu-
late his breathing. Soaked with sweat, he slid out
of bed and put himself under a cool shower in the
guest bedroom so he wouldn't wake his wife.

Water coursing over him, he stood, head bent,
palms pressed against the tile as the brisk tem-
perature of the water cooled his skin. When the
hard spray had banished the worst of the fog, he
stepped out of the shower and dried off.

Wrapping a towel around his waist, he walked
out onto the terrace, the lingering fragments of

his dream evaporating as the pink fingers of dawn crawled across the sky. They had used to come nightly, his nightmares. He couldn't remember the last time he'd had one.

He watched the sun rise over the hills, a fiery yellow ball that crept into the hazy gray sky. *I'm going to be a father.* It had been the goal, of course, but he hadn't expected it to happen so quickly, not when they hadn't even been trying. His brain, his emotions, needed time to catch up, because they were mixed just as his wife's were.

There was joy, undoubtedly, at something he'd at one point decided might never be his. Bittersweet regret his brother would never have that opportunity. And fear. Fear that what happened before might happen again. The fear of more *loss*.

Losing his unborn child on the heels of Lucia had pushed him into a red zone where any more emotional deficits were too much. Where any more losses could push him over the line. So he'd shut down—refused to feel, and avoided any chance of that happening. In doing so, he had pushed Angelina away when she'd needed him the most—when *she* had been at her most vulnerable. No wonder she was so terrified to do this again.

His jaw locked, a slow ache pulsing beneath his ribs. This time would be different. This time he'd made sure he and Angelina's relationship was built on a solid, realistic foundation of what they were both capable of. He would make sure he kept them on track—he would be the steady, protective force she needed as they went through this pregnancy together.

If he worried his emotions for his wife were wandering into dangerous territory—into that red zone he avoided—that his efforts to exorcise her power over him weren't having any effect at all, he would just have to make sure he was extra-vigilant he never crossed that all-important line.

Angelina awoke to the sensually delicious smell of coffee and spicy, hedonistic male. "Breakfast," her husband intoned in her ear, his sexy, raspy tone sending a shiver up her spine, "is served."

She wasn't sure which she wanted to inhale more—him or the coffee. She opened her eyes to find him dressed and clean-shaven. The kiss he pressed to her lips was long, leisurely, the kind that squeezed her heart. Curling her fingers around his nape, she hung on to the magic for as long as possible.

He finally released her, sprawling on the bed. "I bought pastries in the village," he said, gesturing to the tray he'd tucked beside her.

"Is that a chocolate croissant?"

"What do you think?"

Yum. Her husband knew all of her weaknesses. She picked up her espresso and took a sip. Eyed him. Not as bright-eyed and bushy-tailed as she'd first imagined with those dark shadows under his eyes. "Were you up last night? I thought I heard you."

"I woke early." He plucked a croissant off the plate. "An annoying habit I can't seem to get rid of."

She watched him over the rim of her coffee cup as he inhaled the croissant. "I had a thought on the walk back," he said.

She lifted a brow.

"We're going to have to renovate the Belmont locations before we fold them into the Ricci chain. Your clientele is a perfect match. Why not open Carmichael Creations boutiques in them?"

"You haven't even landed them yet. Aren't you getting a little ahead of yourself?"

"It will happen. It's a perfect marriage of brands, don't you think?"

He was serious about this. Her heart contracted. Once she would have given anything to hear him say that. To know he believed in her work that much. But their child needed to take precedence now.

"That's a big compliment," she said carefully, "but I have more business than I can handle at the moment and I want to remain hands-on. Plus, with the baby, I think we'll have our hands full."

"True." His brow creased. "I suggested the hotel boutiques because you've always said you wanted a partnership between us. But the point is for you to be happy, Angelina. That's what I want for you."

A glow inside her sparked, grew to almost scary proportions. She'd never imagined they could be this good. This *amazing* together.

She didn't want to be afraid of loving him anymore. She wanted to trust that this was going to work out, that they were meant to be together, just like he'd said that night in the Hamptons. Taking that last step, however, making herself completely vulnerable, was painfully hard.

His eyes darkened with a sensual heat that made her pulse leap. He nodded toward the half-eaten croissant in her hand. "You going to eat that?"

She shook her head. Put it down. He reached for her, covered her mouth with his in a kiss that was pure heat. Pure possession. She relaxed her grip on the sheets as he stripped them off her, working his way down her body, tasting, idolizing every inch of her.

It was the most leisurely, spine-tinglingly good buildup he'd ever lavished on her. The most perfect thing she'd ever experienced. By the time he joined their bodies, she was so far gone she was never coming back.

Mouth at her ear, his hand closing possessively over her breast, he started to move, seducing her with words as well as with his body. Heart stretching with the force of what she felt for him, she refused to consider the possibility her husband would never love her. She was through sabotaging her happiness.

CHAPTER ELEVEN

THE WEEKS FOLLOWING her trip to Italy were as busy as Angie had expected as she caught up on the backlog of commissions that had come in. She ploughed through the work with the help of her fellow designers, knowing it was a *good* problem to have—growing pains for a business that seemed to have come into its own.

Burying herself in her work allowed her to achieve her other goal of putting her pregnancy into a manageable box and not let the fears eating away at the fringes of her psyche take control. The doctor had confirmed her pregnancy upon their return home, giving her a clean bill of health. She wasn't going to fret about it. Or at least she was *telling* herself that.

Her husband, however, had clearly elected to take the opposite strategy. Although he was giving her the time to work he'd promised her, he had been monitoring her eating and sleeping habits like a hawk, enforcing periods of rest. When he happened to be around, that was. Ever since they'd come home, he had been working day and night to close the Belmont deal. Add to that another acquisition Franco was negotiating that required her husband's counsel and Lorenzo wasn't doing any eating or sleeping himself.

She knew it was an inordinately busy time, but the feeling that their life was sliding into its former self was growing stronger with every day. Their bond was too new, too nascent, not to allow the warning signals to affect her.

Another long day at the studio behind her, she walked into the penthouse just after eight, kicked off her shoes and made herself a cup of tea. Carrying it into the living room, she sat reading a book while she waited for her husband. But the book failed to keep her attention.

Weeks like this were the worst when Lorenzo was gone for nights on end. Old fears crept around her unsuspecting edges, insecurity set in. Given their dinners together at home had vaporized with her husband's insane schedule and he refused to wake her up when he came to bed so late, she didn't even have the comfort his passionate love-making offered, that seemed to make any obstacle seem surmountable.

The minutes ticked by, her agitation rising. Perhaps now that Lorenzo had had his fill of her, now that he'd gotten everything he wanted, he would lose interest again. Perhaps whatever client he was out wining and dining tonight was a convenient excuse to stay away. Perhaps the emotional distance she'd sensed in him since Portofino was a reality.

The clock struck ten. Discarding the book, she decided to take matters into her own hands. To be proactive rather than reactive. To take control of her relationship, something she hadn't done the last time.

In her bedroom, she dug out the lingerie she'd bought earlier that week and slipped it on. The sexy cream-and-black baby doll that just covered her pertinent assets was fairly indecent. She stared at herself in the mirror, rosy color stinging her cheeks. The cream lace bodice did nothing to hide the bold thrust of her nipples, the silk encasing her curves a seductive caress that was pure temptation.

She pulled the elastic from her hair and let it fall around her shoulders the way her husband liked it. A slow smile curved her mouth. *If this didn't bring him running, nothing would.*

Lorenzo arrived back at the table at the trendy restaurant in the meatpacking district, where he and his CMO were entertaining his Japanese business partners to find his phone sitting on his chair.

An amused smile curved his CMO's mouth. "Figured you might not want the whole table seeing that," he said, nodding toward the phone. He leaned closer. "PS—I'd go home if I were you."

Lorenzo glanced at the screen. Almost choked on the sip of beer he'd taken. His wife dressed in a piece of lingerie he'd never seen before—an outrageously sexy piece, by any male's standards, occupied the entire screen. Hair loose around her shoulders, the lingerie doing little to hide the dark shadow of her nipples beneath the transparent lace, she was the twenty-first-century version of a pinup poster. *Times ten.*

He glanced at the message.

Are you coming home?

Heat claimed his cheeks. It took very little of his creative ability to imagine peeling that silk off of her. How she would taste under his mouth. He'd thought his crazy social schedule might prove an ideal cooling-off period for the two of them given the depth of the emotion they'd shared in Portofino. But this, *this* was too much to resist.

"You didn't see that," he muttered to his CMO.

"What?" Gerald said innocently. "I'll cover for you if you want to make an exit."

Lorenzo tucked his phone into his pocket. Put his exit strategy into motion. Except his Japanese colleagues were intent on taking in the entertainment the club provided. It would be rude for him to cut the night short.

He texted his wife back.

Hold that thought.

It was close to midnight, however, by the time he walked into the penthouse. Devoid of light, it was cast in shadows. He let out a low oath that turned the silent space blue and threw his jacket on a chair.

Body pulsing with frustration, every ounce of his blood so far south it was never coming back, he reached up and loosened his tie. A flash of movement near the windows caught his eye.

He took in his wife, silhouetted against the New York skyline, the sexy negligee plastered to every centimeter of her voluptuous body.

Her breasts were bigger with the advance of her pregnancy, their lush, creamy expanse drawing his eye. That tantalizing glimpse of nipple beneath sheer, gauzy fabric made his mouth go dry.

"You waited up." His voice was husky, laced with a need he couldn't hide.

"I was on my way to bed."

Chilly. Distinctly chilly. He gathered his wits as he moved toward her. "I tried to get away, but my business colleagues were in from Japan. It would have looked rude to leave."

"It's fine." She crossed her arms over her chest, amplifying the view of the bare flesh he ached to touch.

He reached for her. She stepped back. "I don't think so."

"There was nothing I could have done, Angelina."

"I'm tired. I'm going to bed."

He caught her hand and pulled her to him, content to work his way back into her good graces. Her perfume drifted into his nostrils, a tantalizing tease that stroked the heat in him higher. "Clearly you're angry," he murmured. "Let me make it up to you. I'm so hot for you, *cara mia*. I will make it so good."

She lifted her vibrant blue gaze to his. "No."

He blinked. "What do you mean 'no'? You sent me a photo of you in lingerie."

"That offer expired an hour ago."

"You are my wife," he barked. "Offers don't expire."

A mutinous set of her lips. "This one just did. Maybe next time I'll be a compelling enough attraction that you will be home before midnight. Maybe next time you won't blow off those dinners *you* insisted on. Maybe when I remember what my husband *looks like*, the offer will be available for redemption."

He scowled. "You are being completely unfair."

She shook her head. "This *is* history repeating itself, Lorenzo. I don't like it, and I'm not imagining it this time."

He drew his brows together. "It's nothing like

the past. We have been great together. We're talking, we're communicating. Just because you have hurt feelings that I didn't jump when you sent me that photo doesn't mean I'm ignoring you. It means I was *busy*."

Her eyes darkened to a stormy, gray blue. "Just because you've had a few drinks and you're hot for a booty call doesn't mean you get to act like a child when it doesn't go your way. Learn your lesson and maybe next time it will work out for you."

Dio, but she was beautiful when she was angry. He loved this strong, sexy version of his wife—it turned him hard as a rock. The problem was, he needed her to give so he could get his hands on her.

"Bene." He lifted his palms in a conciliatory gesture. "I've learned my lesson. Mission accomplished. You've made your point." He trained his gaze on hers, hot, deliberate. "What would you like me to do? Get down on my knees and beg?"

Her confident swagger faltered, a blaze of uncertainty staining her beautiful eyes. He took a step closer. "Just say yes," he murmured, raking her from head to toe. "While I'm there, I'd be happy to indulge you. Mouth, hands, name your pleasure."

A blaze of sensual heat fired her eyes before the ice made a swift reappearance. "I am not a possession to be used and discarded according to your whims."

"You've said that before," he murmured, his good mood rapidly dissipating. "I find it as objectionable as I did the first time. That is *not* what this is, Angelina. These are extraordinary circumstances trying to land this Belmont deal."

"There will always be another deal…another pot of gold at the end of the rainbow. It never stops, Lorenzo. It never will."

"It will. Once we land Belmont, I will be able to breathe again."

She shook her head. "I've watched my mother go through this a thousand times, wondering when my father will deign to pay attention to her again, always putting her second, *third*, if he happened to be having an affair at the time. I've lived through it with you. I won't repeat these hot and cold patterns again—that roller-coaster ride we do so well."

"I am *not* your father." Irritation edged his voice.

"And I've put you first every time since we've been back together in case you hadn't noticed."

"Yes," she agreed, "you have. Which is why I'm speaking up. Because we've built such a great thing together...because I refuse to see things go back to the way they were."

He shook his head. "You're being too sensitive."

"No, I'm not."

He crossed his arms over his chest, too tired, too frustrated to know how to respond. He was giving her all he had and still she wanted more.

Her lashes lowered. "I need sleep. I have a long day tomorrow."

He let her go, refusing to run after her, tongue wagging, like some desperate fool, despite the way he burned for her. Pouring himself a glass of water, he collapsed into a chair, too wired to sleep even though he couldn't remember the last time he had enjoyed that particular human luxury.

Things *would* get better after he landed Belmont. His wife was completely overreacting—a guilt trip he didn't need when making sure she was okay, that she and their baby were healthy, had been his primary obsession amidst the insanity of his life.

He sat back in the chair. Downed a long swallow of water. His wife's indignation, quite honestly, was the least of his problems. Losing the Belmont deal was a real possibility. It was becoming more and more clear the branding issue might be a deal breaker. The business pages were ripe with speculation on the potential megamerger, Ricci stock was on a roller-coaster ride, the board meeting was looming and he needed to get Erasmo Bavaro, the Bavaro scion, onside. But the Bavaro brothers weren't offering access to their father. He had to play the situation very, very carefully and it was driving him mad.

Oh, the world wouldn't end if the deal fell apart, he conceded, but Ricci's stock and reputation would take a serious hit. Confidence would be shaken. And it would be his fault.

I am beginning to think your ambition has got the best of you on this one.

A nerve throbbed at his temple, his fingers tightening around the glass. Had his father been right? Had he finally overstepped himself? Gotten too confident? Cocky?

He rested his head against the back of the chair and closed his eyes. His culpability was a moot point at this stage. All that mattered was getting the deal done. Pulling it out of the ashes.

As for his wife? He'd never promised her perfection—had warned her this was who he was. He'd vowed to be there for her and he would. But perhaps she was right. Perhaps he'd dropped the ball on his promise to be present of late, had let their dinners together slide.

He could rectify that—take her out for dinner tomorrow night. Calm the waters at home.

CHAPTER TWELVE

IT WAS GOING to be a late night.

Angie set the almost completed, black-and-white diamond bracelet on her workbench, sat back in her chair and rubbed her eyes. *Almost there* wasn't good enough when the bracelet was due to one of Manhattan's most noted philanthropists tomorrow, a woman who could make or break her reputation. And since she had already pushed the delivery date back because of her trip to Europe, then had to wait for some stones to be delivered, it needed to get done tonight.

She headed for the coffee machine, thinking maybe java might perk her up. But she suspected what was really bothering her was the fact that although her husband had made an effort to reinstate their dinners at home whenever his schedule permitted, although he was making an effort to be *physically* present, he had become even more emotionally distant over the last couple of weeks.

Keeping the faith, believing in them, was growing increasingly difficult when not knowing if he'd ever love her was burning a hole in her soul. She wanted him to say those three words so badly, it was almost painful. But she knew if he ever did, and it wasn't a given he would, it would take time.

"Do you want me to stay and work with you tonight?" Serina threw her a glance as she put on her coat.

Angie poured herself a cup of coffee. "You have a date." She gave the diminutive blonde an amused look. "That exciting is he?"

Serina made a face. "Friends set us up."

"Then you should definitely go. That's how all the good matches are made."

She wasn't so sure how love at first sight was going to work out for her.

Picking up her coffee, she nursed the steaming cup between her hands. "I have to finish Juliette Baudelaire's bracelet. The clasp I'd envisioned isn't working."

She and Serina conferred on the issue, the other designer agreeing her current design wouldn't work. They tossed around a couple of alternatives, then Serina headed out for her date.

No sooner had Angie settled into her work than her cell phone rang—it was her husband's name on the caller ID.

"Yes," she purred, craving a taste of his raspy, delicious voice to ease her jagged emotions. "I thought you had to work late."

"Marc Bavaro's invited us to the opera tonight. I need you to come."

No hello. No preamble. No sexy rasp. Cool, rapid-fire words thrown at her with that hint of edge he'd been wearing all week.

She bit her lip. "I can't. I'm sorry. I have a bracelet due to an important client in the morning."

"It's a bracelet. Not life or death. Finish it tomorrow."

She stiffened. "It's *due* tomorrow. I've already put her off once because of Marc Bavaro."

"A few hours isn't going to make a difference. Stop being so contrary and get ready. I'll be there in fifteen minutes to pick you up."

The line went dead. She stared at the phone. Had he just called her *contrary*? *Dismissed* her like that?

She put down the phone. Took a couple of deep breaths. Seriously considered calling him back and telling him what he could do with his opera invitation. Except Marc Bavaro was driving him crazy. She could see it on his face when he walked in the door at night…in the dark circles under his eyes he was wearing like a badge. He was under immense pressure to close this deal and the strain was showing.

She exhaled a long breath. Even though her own work would suffer, she would *not* be the one to sabotage their relationship this time.

Juliette's nearly done bracelet glittered on her desk. She supposed she could send her an email and let her know it would be done in the morning, afternoon at the latest. Surely that would be fine?

Decision made, she sent the email and gathered up her things, her animosity growing by the minute. By the time Lorenzo pulled up at the sidewalk in front of her studio, her blood was boiling.

"Ciao." He leaned toward her to give her a kiss when she got into the car. She gave him her cheek instead. His ebony gaze narrowed. "What?"

"If you don't know what, you don't deserve an answer."

He eyed her. "Is it because I called you contrary?" She didn't deign to respond to that.

A muttered oath. "It's one night, Angelina."

She turned a furious gaze on him. "I have a commission due tomorrow. How would you feel if I insisted you attend a party with me when you had a security filing the next day? I can just see you now—'Pff, it's just a security filing...the lawyers have this. Be right with you, honey.'"

"Now you're being ridiculous."

She turned to look out the window.

He gave up after that, getting them home in record time. She changed into a cap-sleeved, navy classic sheath dress, adding elegant gold sandals and jewelry to spice it up. Lorenzo looked devastatingly handsome in a dark suit, white shirt and an ice-blue tie he had clearly put on to match her dress, but she was in no mood to acknowledge it.

They met up with Marc and Penny outside the stunningly beautiful Metropolitan Opera House, with its white travertine stone facade and five massive, graceful arches that, lit up at night, made it a sight to see. It had always been one of Angie's favorite places to go for its sheer magnificence. Her first trip there, to see a ballet as a little girl, had been full of wide-eyed wonder. But tonight she was too annoyed to register much other than the fact that she was itching to shrug off the hand her husband held at her back, but couldn't.

They shared a cocktail with the other couple in one of the bars. Sparkling water, sadly, for Angie, when a glass of wine might have mellowed her out. She focused all her attention on the Belmont CEO and his girlfriend, ignoring her husband completely, to the point where Penny jokingly asked her if Lorenzo was in the doghouse as they settled into their seats in the Belmont box to watch Puccini's *La Bohème*.

She denied it, of course. Made a joking comment that Penny would see what it was like when the honeymoon phase was over. Lorenzo must have heard it with that laser-sharp hearing of his because his face turned dark. A mistake, she recognized, as the whisper of a chill rose up her spine. She had insulted his male pride.

She focused on the performance. He had earned that one.

La Bohème was one of her favorites, but tonight it couldn't have been a worse choice. The story of Mimi and Rodolfo, the fiery, star-crossed lovers, sung to perfection by the visiting Italian soprano and her American tenor—had always moved her.

But tonight, given her rocky emotions, her inse-curities about her and Lorenzo, it affected her in a way she couldn't hide. By the time the two lov-ers decided to stay together in the face of Mimi's heartbreaking illness at the end of the third act, her imminent death on the horizon, tears were running down her face.

Lorenzo put a hand on her thigh. She ignored him, kept her eyes focused on the stage. When the act came to a close, she rooted around desperately in her bag for a tissue, a necessity at the opera, and *dammit*, how could she have forgotten them?

Lorenzo shoved the handkerchief from his front pocket into her hand. "Excuse us, will you?"

"What are you doing?" she whispered as he grabbed her arm and propelled her out of the box.

A tight, intense look back. "We are going some-where to talk."

"I don't want to talk."

"Well, that's too bad, *amore mio*, you don't get to choose."

Into the multistoried lobby they went, past the two glorious murals Marc Chagall had painted. Somewhere along the way, Lorenzo dropped the general manager's name. The next thing she knew, he was directing her down a hallway and into an empty dressing room marked Visiting Performers.

Lorenzo twisted the lock on the door and turned to face his wife. What the hell was wrong with her? Watching her cry like that had made him want to crawl out of his skin, because he didn't think all of it had to do with the admittedly heart-breaking opera.

Angie swept her hand around the room, dominated by the sofa that sat along one wall and a dressing table and mirror on the other. "We can't be in here."

"I was just told we could." He crossed his arms over his chest. "Explain to me why you are so angry, *cara*. I asked you to do me a favor. You know how important this deal is to me. What's the problem?"

She jammed her hands on her hips, eyes flashing. "You *ordered* me to come. You know how important my career is to me and yet you completely discounted my work. The bracelet I'm creating is for Juliette Baudelaire—a huge commission, particularly if she spreads the word to her friends. It's not just a bracelet, it's a *stepping stone* in my career. And yet here I am, not delivering on time—*twice*—because of you and your needs."

His irritation came to a sudden, sliding halt. "I had no idea it was for her."

"*How could you?* You hung up on me before I had a chance to tell you."

He muttered an oath. Pushed a palm over his brow. "*Mi dispiace.* I'm sorry. I wasn't thinking when I called you. I was behind, annoyed because I had prior commitments I, too, had to cancel."

She hugged her arms around herself. Glared at him. He scowled back. "You," he said, waving a hand at her, "are so emotional tonight. What's going on? Is it the pregnancy effect?"

The daggers in her eyes would have sliced him to shreds if they'd been real. "*You*, Lorenzo Ricci, are so oblivious, so *emotionally unaware* sometimes it blows my mind."

He didn't think that was fair. He thought he was *very* emotionally aware at times and had been with her *a lot* lately. They were talking. *Communicating.* Being honest with each other. The last couple of weeks had just been particularly brutal.

The thought vaporized from his head as his wife headed for the door. Moving with a swiftness born of his superior height and muscle, he made it there at the same time she did. Jamming his palm against the wood, he looked down at his very beautiful, very angry wife.

"We aren't done talking."

"Oh, yes, we are."

"No," he said deliberately, "we aren't."

She crossed her arms over her chest. "What else would you like to say?"

"I'd like to say I'm sorry again. I sincerely feel badly that I did not check to see what it was you were working on. If I'd known, I would have come by myself."

Her stormy blue gaze softened.

"I would also like to know how I am being *emotionally unaware*."

She pursed her lips. "You're kidding, right?"

"No." He frowned. "I thought we had the pregnancy thing out in the open. We're dealing with it."

"It's not that." She shook her head. "Women cannot *stand* when a man plays the hormone card, Lorenzo. It's like waving a red flag in front of a bull."

"Oh. *Certo*," he said, nodding. "I will remember that for the future. I had no idea. I thought pregnancy hormones were a documented thing."

"*Lorenzo.*" She glared at him. "I'd stop while you're ahead."

"*Bene.*" He snagged an arm around her waist and pulled her close. "Is there anything else you would like to tell me? Why you are so upset?"

Her gaze dropped away from his. "You haven't been emotionally present the last few weeks. I don't know where your head is. I don't know where *we* are. I miss you."

Guilt tied a knot in his chest. In trying to pull back, to not lead them down a path he couldn't go, he'd hurt her.

"I'm sorry." He bent his head and buried his mouth in the curve of her neck. Drank in her irresistible scent. "Things have been crazy. I will do better."

"It's...I—" She sighed. "We should go. Find Marc and Penny."

"Not until you say you're not angry with me anymore." He slid his hands down over her bottom and pulled her closer. "I hate it when you're angry with me."

Tracing the line of her neck with his lips, he

sank his teeth into the cord of her throat where it throbbed against her skin. Her breath hitched. "Fine. I'm not angry at you anymore."

"I'm not convinced." He dragged his mouth up to hers. Pushed his fingers into her hair and kissed her. Dominant, persuasive, he sought to fix whatever was going on with her. To fix *them* in the only way he knew how.

She melted beneath his hands. "Okay," she whispered against his lips. "You're forgiven."

But he was too far gone now, his body pulsing with the need to restore the natural balance of things. Denying himself Angelina was carving a hole inside of him he didn't know how to fill.

He backed her into the wall, pushed his thigh between hers, imprinting her with the throbbing evidence of his need. She gasped. *"Lorenzo."*

"What?"

"We can't do this here."

"Why not?" He slicked his tongue over her lush bottom lip, tasting her. "You liked it in Portofino. The element of risk…"

"Yes, but—"

He delved inside the sweetness of her mouth. Made love to her with his tongue like he wanted to do to her body. Her bag clattered to the floor, a low moan leaving her throat. Lust coursing through him, he nudged her legs farther apart and swept her dress up her thighs. She was damp when he cupped her between her legs, as turned on as he was.

He ran his palm over the hot, wet silk that covered her. Moved it aside to find her slick and ready for him.

"I need to have you," he rasped.

Her stormy blue gaze locked with his. *"Yes."*

He stroked her. Readied her. She made more of those sexy sounds at the back of her throat, arching into his hand. Shallow strokes of his fingers inside her tight channel to tease, insistent circles against the tight bundle of nerves at the heart of her with his thumb. Throwing her head back, she said his name in a broken voice that ripped right through him.

Urging one of her legs around his waist, he released himself from his pants, pushed aside the wet silk and entered her with a hard, urgent thrust. She gasped, the sensation of her tight, velvet warmth gripping his swollen flesh indescribable. It had never been so good.

"Okay?" he murmured.

"Yes."

Bending his knees, he drove up inside of her with an urgent desire that annihilated anything but the need to have her. His erection pounded in time with his heartbeat, his control shredding. He captured her hand in his and brought her fingers to the hard nub that gave her pleasure.

"Touch yourself," he whispered. "Come with me, Angelina."

She closed her eyes. Rotated her fingers against her flesh. He kept his hand over hers, absorbing the tiny quakes that went through her. Held on to the very threads of his control while she pleasured herself. When she was close, when the deeper shudders came, moving from her through him, he gripped her hip tighter and stroked deeper, setting a hard, wild rhythm that blew his brain apart.

His body tightened, swelled, his breathing hoarse in the silence of the room. In perfect sync, they came together in a soul-shaking release like none he'd ever experienced before.

Mouth buried in her neck, he held her as her legs gave out. He wasn't sure how long they stayed like that, wrapped around each other, before he recovered enough to straighten and push back.

Bracing a palm against the wall, he leaned in to kiss her, to acknowledge what that had just been. His heart stopped in his chest at the tears streaming down her cheeks.

"Angelina?" He cupped her face with his hands. "What is it?"

She shook her head. Pushed away as she straightened her clothes. "It's nothing. I'm emotional from the performance."

The bell sounded to end the intermission. He ignored it, focusing on his wife's tear-streaked face as he zipped himself up. "It's a hell of a lot more than that."

She swiped the tears from her face with the backs of her hands.

"Angelina," he roared. "Out with it."

She bent and scooped her purse off the floor. Straightening, she rested her blue gaze on his. "I'm in love with you, Lorenzo. Silly me, I forgot the rules."

CHAPTER THIRTEEN

LORENZO'S JAW DROPPED. "ANGIE——"

The bell rang again. His wife turned, unlocked the door and walked out. Blood pounding at his temples, he straightened his shirt and followed her out.

How he sat through the last act, he wasn't sure. It was like someone was driving nails into his head in some kind of ancient torture. When it was finally, mercifully over, they bid Marc and Penny a good night and acquired the car from the valet. Neither of them spoke in the loaded silence of the car.

The penthouse was in shadows as they entered, Manhattan spread out before them in all its glory. He threw his jacket on a chair and headed straight for the bar and a stiff shot of whiskey.

Angelina kicked off her shoes. When she headed for the bedroom, he pointed to the sofa. *"Sit."*

She lifted her chin. "What's the point? I know

you can't tell me what I want to hear. You would have said it to me in that dressing room if you could."

It was a truth he couldn't deny. He wanted to— he wanted to tell her everything she wanted to hear if it would wipe the hurt from her eyes, but he'd promised her honesty and they'd come too far to give each other anything but.

He set down the whiskey. Pushed a hand through his hair. "To lose someone you love like I loved Lucia changes a person. You *know* too much. Things you should never have to know… things that make you question everything you once took for granted—the *natural order* of things. It isn't a faith I'll ever have again. Loving someone like that isn't something I'm *capable* of doing. But it doesn't mean I don't care for you. You know I do."

Her eyes grew suspiciously bright. "Not capable," she asked quietly, "or simply unwilling to try?"

He lifted a shoulder. "It is who I am."

The brightness in her eyes dissolved on a blaze of fire. "You know what I think, Lorenzo? I think it's a cop-out, this 'I am who I am' line of yours.

Saying you can't love again is easier than making yourself vulnerable…easier than exposing yourself to the potential for pain, so you choose not to go there. You choose to believe you are incapable of love."

He shook his head. "I won't tell you lies. We promised each other that. But what we have, Angelina—is something *more* than love. What we have is based on rationality, on that great partnership you've always wanted, on the affection we have for each other. It is *real*. It's what's going to make this marriage work. *Last*."

She wrapped her arms around herself. Turned to look out the window. He closed the distance between them, curled his fingers around her shoulder and turned her to him. "We have a good thing," he said softly, "an electric connection—a special connection. The kind that rarely, if ever, comes along. We will be great parents to our child because we know the gift it is. What more could you ask for?"

"The love of a lifetime," she said quietly. "You had yours. Maybe I want mine. Maybe *this* isn't enough."

His stomach contracted, her words sucking

the breath from him. He inhaled, dragged in a breath. Searched for something, *anything* to say. But he knew what she was saying was true. She deserved to have that untainted love—everything he couldn't give her. But he'd thought he could make her happy by giving her everything else. He should have known it would never be enough.

Naked pain wrote itself across her beautiful face. "I have to go to bed. I need to deliver that bracelet to Juliette tomorrow and I still have to figure out the clasp."

He watched her leave the room, a heavy, hollow ache in his chest, because he wasn't sure he could fix this. It was the one thing he *couldn't* fix.

Bleary-eyed from a restless, sleepless night, Angie forced herself into the studio shortly after her husband left for the office, putting on coffee just as the birds were beginning to sing.

She sat down at her desk with a cup of the strong brew, numbly processing the events of the night before. She hadn't meant to confront Lorenzo. She'd meant to give him time. But somewhere along the way, her emotions so raw, it had just come tumbling out. Maybe it had been the way she'd been desperately begging for crumbs in that dressing room when they'd made love, terrified they were falling apart again—needing to know they were okay. How they were once again using sex to solve problems they couldn't fix.

Her heart throbbed. How could she have allowed herself to make the same mistake she'd made the first time around? To think, on some instinctual level, her husband might love her but not be able to admit it?

It was never going to happen even if he did. And she knew, even if she convinced herself that what they had was enough, even if she bought his whole line about them being *more* than love, she'd end up hating him for never offering her what she so desperately wanted. Because she wanted it—she did. The love she'd never had. The love she knew they could have together.

She deserved it. She had always deserved it. She was *worthy* of it. She knew that now. And what hurt the most was her husband was capable of it. He'd loved Lucia once. He just wasn't going to offer it to her.

The ache in her insides grew. She wanted to be the light in Lorenzo's life, his everything as he was becoming to her. As he'd always been to her. This wasn't her sabotaging them, it was *him* sabotaging them.

She took another sip of her coffee. Pulled herself together. Allowing her work to slide wasn't going to make this any easier.

A return email from Juliette Baudelaire sat in her inbox. A short, curt reply.

Not to worry. I found another piece to wear to the luncheon. Given that, I no longer require the bracelet.

Her heart sank. Thousands of dollars of diamonds had gone into that bracelet. But that wasn't even the point—she could resell it. The point was that Juliette knew everyone and loved to talk. Her reputation was going to take a bump for this, she knew it in her bones.

She sat back in her chair. Closed her eyes.

"You okay?" Serina breezed in and hung up her coat.

No, she decided, tears stinging her eyes. She was most definitely not okay. But she wasn't going to let that man take her apart again. Not this time.

* * *

"Do you want the good news or the bad?"

Lorenzo eyed his lawyer, his mood vile. "Why don't you start with the bad and work up to the good?"

"The Belmont lawyers called while you were in your meeting. They want to meet tomorrow in Miami to discuss some final issues."

Lorenzo's fingers curled tight around the toy football he held. Marc Bavaro was going to be the one to finally make him snap. He could feel it.

"What's the good news?"

"The meeting will be at Erasmo Bavaro's place."

He sat forward. "That is good news." But *Miami*…tomorrow?

Cris eyed his scowl. "Please tell me we're saying yes."

"Bene." He blew out a breath. "Make it happen. We need to get this done. But I swear this is the swan song."

His lawyer left. Lorenzo sat back in his chair, his satisfaction at finally moving this game to a place he was comfortable with only slightly improving his foul mood. His volatility had as much to do with his wife's ultimatum as it did with

Bavaro's antics. With the fact that she'd thrown that explosive three-word phrase at him, pushed him for things he couldn't give and destroyed the delicate, satisfactory stasis he'd had going on. Backed him into a corner with nowhere left to go.

Flying to Miami tomorrow seemed unwise given the current state of affairs. But what could he do? If he didn't get Erasmo Bavaro on board this deal was as good as dead.

Swinging his feet off his desk, he threw the things he'd need for Miami in his briefcase and headed home to solve his problem. His wife was making herself some hot milk in the kitchen when he walked in.

"How was your day?" he asked, setting his briefcase on the floor. *Reintroducing stasis.*

"Busy." She put down the cup and rubbed her palms against her temples.

"Did you get Juliette's bracelet done?"

She lifted her gaze to his, her face expression-less. "I lost the commission. She went out and bought something else to wear."

Uh-oh. This did not bode well for the conversation they needed to have. "I'm sorry," he said quietly, "that was wrong of me. But we still need to talk. Work this out."

She shook her head. "*You* need to work this out. I know how I feel."

A twinge of unease spread through him. "What are you saying?"

"I'm saying I can't live without love. I can't stay in this marriage unless you can offer that to me." She shook her head, teeth sinking into her lip. "You have made me face up to my past, Lorenzo. You have made me see how I run from the things that scare me so I won't get hurt. Well, I'm not running now. I *deserve* to be happy. I deserve to have all of you. And if you can't offer that to me, it will break my heart, but I will walk away because you've also helped me realize how strong I am."

His chest clenched. "You're willing to throw everything we have away because I can't say three words?"

Her eyes darkened. "It's more than that and you know it. I've watched you struggle over the past few weeks. I know how hard this is for you. But I can't live with pieces of you. It would break my heart. We would end up hating each other. You know we would."

"No, I do not know that." His fists tightened at his sides. "This is not negotiable, Angelina. You are carrying my child. Our fate was sealed the day that happened."

"No, it wasn't." She shook her head. "You have your heir. We will work that out. But you can't have me. Not like this. I must have been insane to ever agree to that deal we made."

"You aren't walking out on me again." His voice was pure frost. "You know the conditions I attached to this."

"You won't do it." Her eyes were stark in a face gone white. "The other thing I have learned is that under that armor you wear is the man I met. The man I would have given anything to have. *He* wouldn't let my family suffer. He would not hurt me."

Blood pounded in his ears, a red-hot skewer of rage lancing through him. "Try me, *cara*. Just try me. You think you can leave me and cozy up to *Byron* again with my child inside you? It will never happen. I will drag this divorce out for all eternity."

She stared at him as if she couldn't believe what she was hearing. He couldn't believe what he was saying. But the rage driving him didn't care who or what he hurt.

She didn't flinch. Held his gaze. "Byron and I were over when I realized I was still in love with you and you damn well know it."

He raked a hand through his hair. Struggled to see past his fury. "I have to go to Miami tomorrow. Erasmo Bavaro has agreed to meet with us. We will talk about this when I get back."

"I won't be here." The pain staining her blue eyes nearly tore him in two. "I know who I am, Lorenzo, and I know I can't do this."

She turned on her heel and walked toward the bedroom.

Corrosive anger roped his heart. "Goddammit, Angelina, get back here."

She kept going.

In the center of the red zone, well aware of where it could take him, he downed the rest of the whiskey. He could not afford to go there, not now with the most important deal of his life hanging in the balance. Not ever when his wife was asking more of him than he could ever give.

CHAPTER FOURTEEN

ERASMO BAVARO WAS as cagey as his son Marc and as animated as Diego, a fearsome combination in a silver-haired fox who reminded Lorenzo of his father.

It would have been fascinating to see the two titans face off in their heyday, but on a brilliantly sunny afternoon in Miami, with the Bavaro scion's palatial poolside terrace the backdrop for the negotiations, his focus was on pulling Erasmo into the twenty-first century.

Erasmo, for his part, looked content to stay right where he was. Flanked by his lawyers at the long, olive wood table, coolly dressed in a flamboyant short-sleeved shirt and trousers, he swept a palm over his neatly trimmed, salt-and-pepper goatee and eyed Lorenzo. "Let me tell you a story," he said in a deeply accented voice. "Perhaps it will help you to understand where I'm coming from.

"The night we opened the Belmont in South Beach in 1950, we had the most popular blues singer on the planet, Natalie Constantine, lined up to play. Near the end of her set, Arturo Martinez walked onto the stage and joined her for the last two songs."

Arturo Martinez. The Spanish megastar who had sold more albums in those days than any singer alive.

"They closed out the night in the piano bar. Two legends. Such was the mystique of the Belmont legacy. You could not have paid to be there that night."

"They were great days," Lorenzo acknowledged. "I wish I had been there that night. But that time has come and gone, Erasmo. It's time for the mantle to be passed on. All good things must come to an end."

"Speaks the man who puts money above meaning." The Bavaro patriarch lifted a brow. "Can I share something with you, Ricci? Money will not give your life meaning when you are my age. Money will not keep you warm at night. Money won't nourish your soul when you've spent fifty years in this business and every boardroom table looks like the rest. *Meaning* will. Your legacy will."

"Speaks a man perhaps lost in his own senti-mentality..."

Erasmo dipped his head. "Perhaps. But I would prefer to be remembered as a man who built things rather than tore down the work of others."

The rebuke stung his skin. Lorenzo lifted the glass of potent, exotic rum his host had unearthed from his cellar to his lips and took a sip. It burned a slow path through his insides, but it didn't take the sting out of the old man's words. Nor did the fact that his wife, who'd walked out on him *again*, felt the same way.

Angelina thought he'd sold his soul for his success. Bartered it for an escape from the guilt he refused to acknowledge—the feelings he refused to address. The ironic thing was, in that moment, as the cast of lawyers digressed into legalese he couldn't be bothered to follow, he couldn't remember why this deal had ever been so important to him. Why he was sitting here haggling over a name when the most important thing in his life was back in New York. *Refusing to take his calls.*

And why would she? Regret sat like a stone in

his stomach. He'd threatened to withdraw his funding of Carmichael Company if she left...to drag their divorce out for all eternity. Had he really thought that would make her stay?

His insides coiled tight. What the hell was wrong with him? He had no idea what he was doing anymore. Hadn't since Angelina had laid all his truths out for him and challenged him to do the same. Since a phone call in the middle of a meeting in Shanghai had obliterated the life he'd known and had him planning a funeral rather than the family he and Lucia had envisioned.

He rubbed a palm across his forehead, a low throb sitting just below his skin. He'd told Angelina he wasn't capable of loving again. Had meant it. But watching her walk out on him a second time, watching her lay her heart on the line about how she felt about him had done something to him. If his wife, who'd been hurt so many times it was a scar on her soul, could be that courageous, what did that make him? A *coward*?

The tightness in his chest deepened. He'd allowed her to walk away, continued to pretend he didn't feel the things he did for her because then he wouldn't have to face the truth. That he loved her. Had loved her from the first moment he'd laid eyes on her. That he was so afraid of losing someone else, so afraid of losing *her*, so angry at her still for leaving him, he didn't have the guts to put himself out there. To tell her how he felt.

His heart punched through his chest. *Blaming yourself for Lucia's death is easier than making yourself vulnerable again.*

He curled his fingers into his thighs, waiting for the shame, the guilt, to dig its claws into him, to claim him as it always did when he allowed himself to think of that night. But it didn't come. His fear was greater—his fear of losing his wife, the woman who made him whole.

He closed his eyes. What would she think if she knew the true story? That his inability to be present for his wife, to listen to her, the same failings he had brought to his marriage with Angelina, had led to Lucia's death? That *he* was responsible for it?

He finished his drink in a long swig. Set the glass down. What was clear was that he hadn't fulfilled his end of his bargain with his wife. He'd insisted Angelina be an open book, but he hadn't been with her. He owed her the truth, because if he continued to use his guilt as a crutch, to hide from his emotions, he would lose her anyway. And losing his wife, he realized, wasn't an option.

The lawyers droned on. The sun beat down on his head. Perhaps knowing, *accepting* he should have done things differently and forgiving himself for Lucia's death were two separate things. Maybe he needed to forgive himself for being human in the decisions he'd made...maybe that was something he could live with.

He leaned forward, palms on the table. "We will cobrand the hotels," he interjected, cutting through the din. "'The Ricci South Beach, *formerly a Belmont hotel.*' That's as far as I'm willing to take it."

Cristopher gaped at his about-face. Lorenzo stood up. "You have twenty-four hours to give us a response—after that, the deal is dead."

Marc eyed him. "You're walking out?"

"I'm taking a page out of your father's book. I'm finally getting my priorities straight. You've had a year to do that, Bavaro, I'm giving you another twenty-four hours' grace."

Whether he had that with Angelina after the things he'd said to her remained to be seen.

* * *

"Why don't you just take his calls if you're this miserable?"

Angie looked up from her bowl of pasta to find her sister's watchful gaze on her. "Because we both need space. And," she said, dropping the fork in the bowl and pushing it away, "I'm angry at him."

Furious. Lonely. Miserable. But she wasn't about to add fuel to the fire by dragging her sister into this. They were supposed to be having a nice night out at their favorite restaurant, something she desperately needed.

"You know," Abigail said quietly, "Lorenzo called James this afternoon."

She sat up straighter. "*James?* Why?"

"Father is stepping down and making James CEO. Lorenzo's going to come in and work side by side with him to right-side Carmichael Company."

Her jaw dropped. "And I don't know about this why?"

"Apparently it's been in the works for a while, but Father just made the decision this week. According to James, Lorenzo gave Father an ultimatum a few weeks back—step down or he will withdraw his financial support."

"He's good at that," Angie muttered. "Throwing his weight around." She frowned, playing with the straw in her iced tea. "The question is why? He can barely manage his own schedule. How is he going to accommodate this?"

"I don't know," Abigail said softly, her attention on something behind Angie, "but you could ask him. I think your *space* just ran out."

She whipped her head around. Felt the blood drain from her face. Lorenzo, in a silver-gray suit, navy tie and white shirt, stood talking to the hostess. All magnetic, bespoke elegance, the pretty blonde was clearly dazzled by him, her megawatt smile as she pointed to their table blinding.

Angie turned back to her sister, butterflies swarming her stomach. "How did he know I was here?" Her gaze narrowed. "*You* told him."

Abigail sat back in her chair, wineglass in hand. "You just said you're in love with him. Not that that's a news flash. You two need to work things out."

"Traitor," Angie growled. But then her husband was standing beside their table and everything inside her seemed to vibrate with the need to hold him, to have him, she'd missed him so much.

She pressed her lips together. Looked up at him. "What are you doing here?"

He eyed her, his dark stare making her heart thud in her chest. "I've come to get my wife."

Her stomach lurched. "You can't order me around, Lorenzo. I'm done with that."

"It wasn't an order. I'm asking you to come home with me and talk this out."

She sank her teeth into her lip. "Lorenzo—"

"Please." The husky edge to his voice raked her skin. Deepened the ache inside of her to unbearable levels.

She took a deep breath. "I'm not sure it's a good idea."

"You think I don't love you?" he rasped, his gaze holding hers. "What do you think this has all been about, Angelina? Me running after you like a lunatic? Me not being able to forget you? Me acting like a complete jackass? I've been in love with you since the first moment I laid eyes on you. If my behavior hasn't made that clear, I don't know what will."

"He has a point," Abigail said dryly. "As much

as I'm enjoying this spectacular grovel, however, there are at least two tabloid reporters in the house tonight. Perhaps you should hear the man out."

Angie barely heard her, she was so utterly gobsmacked by what her husband had just said. At the truth glimmering in his black eyes. Never had she expected to hear him say those three words. Certainly not in a restaurant full of people now staring at them.

She glanced at her sister. Abigail waved her off with an amused lift of her hand. "I'll have the fudge cake while I imagine being a fly on the wall. *Go.*"

Lorenzo captured her fingers in his and dragged her to her feet. Through the crowded restaurant they went, her half running to keep up with his long strides.

The car sat waiting with the valet. Lorenzo tucked her into the passenger seat, got in and drove home. Angie watched him, head spinning. "What happened in Miami? Did you sign the deal?"

"No. I told Erasmo Bavaro I would cobrand the hotels, that was my final offer, and gave them twenty-four hours to take it or leave it."

"Oh." She frowned. "You said you'd never do that."

"Things change."

"The Bavaros got to you, didn't they?"

"Perhaps. My wife also made it clear she disapproves of my slash-and-burn approach to business."

She eyed him. "Why are you helping James?"

"Because I think Carmichael can be great again, but it needs your brother at the helm. A modern leadership. And," he added, flicking her a glance, "I like the idea of building something again."

"You have no capacity. What if you land Belmont?"

"I will hand it off to the VP I hired last week. It's all part of the plan."

"What plan?"

"To keep you." Quiet words, full of meaning. *Promise.* "It was always about keeping you, Angelina. I just didn't go about it the right way."

Oh. Her heart melted. It was hard to stay angry when he said things like that.

Traffic unusually light, they made it home in minutes. Lorenzo flicked on the lights in the living room, poured them glasses of sparkling water, handed one to Angie and lowered himself into a chair. She curled up in the one opposite him.

"I need to tell you about Lucia," he said quietly. "All of it."

Her heart beat a jagged rhythm. "Lorenzo—"

He held up a hand. "I need to do it."

She sat back, heart in her mouth.

"My trip to Shanghai, the week Lucia died, was an intense trip for me. Three days in and out—nonstop meetings. Lucia wanted to come. I told her no, I wouldn't have any time for her. She was…nervous living in New York. She was from a small village in Italy, she didn't feel safe here. I thought by not taking her with me on that trip, not dragging her through those time zones when we were trying to conceive, she would be better off." His mouth flattened. "I also thought it would help toughen her up. Show her she could do it on her own."

Oh, no. She pressed her fingers to her mouth. The guilt he must feel.

"When the robbers left her alone," he continued, cheekbones standing out like blades, "she called me instead of 911. The call went to my voice mail.

I was in a meeting. When I listened to the message, I lost my mind."

Her throat constricted. "No," she whispered. "Lorenzo, no." Tears welled up in her eyes. She got up, closed the distance between them and slid onto his lap. "It wasn't your fault," she murmured, pressing her lips to his cheek. "Tell me you don't think it was your fault."

The soul-deep wounds in his eyes said otherwise. "I should have respected her fears and taken her with me."

She shook her head. "You were trying to make her *stronger*. You were protecting her in your own way. I know that because you've done it with me. You've pushed me when I needed to be pushed, forced me to face my fears. It's how you care."

His dark lashes swept across his cheeks. "I'm not telling you this to inspire your pity, I'm telling you so you understand me. *Us*. It was never about me still loving Lucia, Angelina. It was about me being consumed by guilt. Me not being able to forgive myself for what I'd done. Me never wanting to feel that pain again."

Hot tears ran down her cheeks. She brushed them away, salt staining her mouth. Finally she understood what drove her husband. Finally she understood *him*. He'd lost the most important thing in his life to a senseless act that could not be explained so he had blamed it on himself instead because, in his mind, he could have prevented it.

She cupped his jaw in her hands. "You have to forgive yourself. You have to accept what happened was beyond your control or you—*we*—will never be whole."

He nodded. "I know that. Watching you walk away from me this week was a wake-up call. I thought I could outrun the past—the guilt. But having to face it or lose you, I realized that wishing I'd made different decisions, acknowledging I've made mistakes, is something apart from forgiveness. That maybe I need to forgive myself for being human. I think it might help me let go."

Her heart stretched with the force of what she felt for him. For the peace she hoped he would find now.

"And then there was you," he said quietly. "Admitting how I felt about you. How angry I still was with you. When you walked away from me the first time, I was just learning to trust, to love again. I *was* in love with you. But I wouldn't admit it—wouldn't allow myself to love you—because I didn't think you were a sure bet. When you left, you proved me right."

Her heart squeezed. "I should never have left. I should have worked through things with you."

He shook his head. "I think it needed to happen. You needed to grow up—to become who you've become. *I* needed to realize who that woman is—to appreciate her. Our timing was off."

Maybe he was right. Maybe it hadn't been their time. Maybe now was.

"Forgive me," he said, pressing his mouth to her temple. "I was a fool to let you walk away a second time…to say those things I didn't mean. If I don't have you, *mi amore*, I am nothing. I am a shell of a man, because you take a part of me with you every time you leave."

Her heart climbed into her throat. "Promise me you will always tell me when you're hurting. Promise me you will always be that open book you talked about and I will."

"Sì," he agreed, lowering his mouth to hers. "No more holding back."

He kissed her then. Passionate and never-ending, it was full of such bone-deep need, such *truth*, it reached inside her and wound its way around her heart, melting the last of the ice. She curled her fingers around the lapels of his jacket and hung on as every bit of the misery of the past week unraveled in the kiss and was swept away.

A sharp nip of her bottom lip brought her back to reality. "That," her husband remarked, "was for ignoring my phone calls this week."

"You deserved it."

"Yes," he agreed throatily, standing and sweeping her up in his arms, "I did. Allow me to demonstrate how very sorry I am."

He carried her through the shadowy penthouse to their bedroom. Dispensing with her dress, he set her on the bed. She watched as he stripped off his clothes, his body showcased to delicious advantage in the close-fitting black hipster briefs he favored.

His eyes turned a smoky black as he stripped them off and joined her on the bed. "You like what you see? Take it, *cara*, I'm all yours."

She straddled his beautiful, muscular body, emotion clogging her throat. "I've missed you," she murmured, leaning over to kiss him. "Nothing is right when I'm not with you. You are my heart, Lorenzo Ricci."

His kiss said the words back. Passionate, perfect, it was everything she knew they were going to be. Because now that they were an open book, now that they had exorcised their last ghost, anything was possible.

Breaking the kiss, she took him inside her slick heat. Gasped when he tilted his hips and filled her with his thick, hard length in a single thrust that stole her breath.

"You can't do it, can you? Let me take control?"

His dark eyes glittered. "You wouldn't have it any other way."

No…she wouldn't. Not in this particular arena.

She let herself drown in his black eyes as he made love to her slowly, languidly, telling her how much he loved her until their breath grew rough and they were both poised on the edge of a release that promised to be spectacular.

"Say it again," she murmured.

"What?"

"That you love me."

His mouth curved. *"Ti amo, angelo mio."*

I love you, my angel.

Her heart wove itself back together. "I love you, too, Lorenzo," she whispered back before he closed his hands around her hips and took her to heaven.

Her first love. Her only love. *Her forever love.*

EPILOGUE

Nassau, Bahamas,
El Paraíso de Mar—the Carmichael Estate

"PAPA!"

A squeal of delight from one of her girls was Angie's first hint that her husband had arrived home in time for the Carmichaels' annual winter party, just as he'd promised, after a week's trip to Italy.

Ready for a shower before the party, she slipped on a robe, tied it around her waist and walked to stand in the doorway of the adjoining bedroom. Her husband stood in jeans and a T-shirt, his bag abandoned, a giggling, excited daughter under each arm as their nanny looked on.

Abelie Lucia and Liliana Ines, their four-year-old identical twins, were playing their usual game.

"Lili," said Abelie, pressing a hand to her chest.

Lorenzo gave her a kiss and set her down. *"E, Abelie,"* he said, giving his other daughter a kiss.

The girls collapsed into gales of laughter. *"Mia Abelie,"* her oldest reproved, wrinkling her nose at her father.

"Ah, sì," Lorenzo said, keeping a straight face. "Silly me."

Her heart swelled, too big, it seemed, for her chest. The arrival of their daughters, the love the four of them shared, had changed her husband. The darkness was gone, replaced by a man who embraced the moment. There were still times when she could tell he was remembering, a sadness would come over him that would perhaps never leave him completely, but those times were few and far between.

"Festa?" Liliana said hopefully, turning her big blue eyes on her father.

"No. This party is for big people. But perhaps you can take your gift to bed with you."

Liliana spotted the brightly colored packages Lorenzo had left on the table. *"Regali,"* she crowed.

Lorenzo handed a package to each of them. Her chubby hands moving as fast as she could maneuver them, Liliana ripped open her gift to find a beautiful, dark-haired doll inside that looked exactly like her. Abelie did the same in a more sedate fashion, as was her personality, discovering an identical doll. A deliberate choice, Angie knew, to avoid the inevitable meltdown if one choice was more popular than another.

The girls oohed and aahed over their dolls. Angie observed her eldest's quieter admiration. It had been Angie's suggestion to name Abelie after Lucia. She'd wanted to honor her memory, to honor her husband's memories, to make it clear Lucia would never be forgotten. Lorenzo, in a very emotional acceptance, had agreed.

Abelie, sharp as a tack, noticed a third present on the table, wrapped in a different paper. *"Mamma?"* she asked.

"Sì."

"Can I open it now?"

Her husband turned to face her, a warm glint filling his dark eyes, the one he reserved exclusively for her. He picked up the gift, prowled toward her and bent and kissed her soundly. The girls devolved into another fit of giggles.

Lorenzo's mouth curved as he set her away from

him. "Off to the bath," he commanded the girls. "I will come in and give you a kiss good-night when you're done."

"E bambole?" Abelie said.

"And your dolls," he agreed. "You," he said, handing the package to Angie, "put this on and meet me downstairs when you're ready. I need to find your brother before the guests arrive."

He was still giving orders, she noted. But tonight she didn't mind. She was too excited to have him home.

She showered while the girls had their bath, applied a light dusting of makeup in her dressing room and slipped on some naughty lingerie as a "welcome home" present for her husband. Opening his gift, she found a sparkly, beaded dress lying in the tissue, an Italian designer label attached.

Her heart contracted. She slid the dress over her head. The material settled over her curves in a whisper of silk, falling to just above her knee, its fit perfect. Exquisitely crafted, it hugged her body like a second skin, a plunging neckline offering a tantalizing glimpse of cleavage. *A very sexy dress.*

She left her hair loose as it had been that magical night she'd met her husband, slipped on high-heeled sandals and spritzed herself with perfume. After kissing the girls good-night, she made her way down the circular stairway to the main floor, the house ablaze with light and the chatter of hundreds of guests.

The Carmichael winter party, never an occasion to be missed, attracted friends and acquaintances from every corner of the globe. Tonight was no exception. Even the Bavaros were here, the two families having formed a close friendship.

Where before there would have been dread in her veins as she stepped out onto the terrace, a rejection of everything this represented, tonight there was only an all-encompassing glow. Her mother was stable and happy. Four years sober, Angie was cautiously optimistic this time her mother would stay healthy. But she'd accepted it was beyond her control. She had her own family now and they were her priority.

She sought out her husband in the thick crowd. It didn't take long because he was exactly where she'd figured he would be—leaning against the bar at the far end of the pool where the band was playing.

Just that little bit aloof, more than a bit untouchable, he looked dazzling in a black tux, his hair slicked back from his face. Her breath caught in her chest. Would she always react to him this way? As if her world had turned on its axis?

She took the last few steps toward him, his dark gaze tracking her. Coming to a stop in front of him, she rested a hand on the bar and looked up into his arresting face. "That's an awfully serious look for a party."

The forbidding line of his mouth softened. "Maybe I'm a serious man."

"Maybe you should stop brooding," she suggested huskily, "and ask me to dance. Unless, of course, you intend on holding up that bar all night."

A sensual glitter entered his gaze. "I think that's an offer I can't refuse, Mrs. Ricci."

Reaching behind him, he produced two glasses of champagne. Glasses in their hands, they took to the dance floor, soaking up a perfect Bahamian night, the scent of a dozen tropical blooms in the air.

Eventually they drifted off into the gardens, majestic palm trees swaying overhead. "I do believe you have dishonorable intentions," she teased when her husband drew back and set her empty glass on the stone wall beside his.

"Certo," he agreed, a heated promise in his eyes. "But first I have something for you."

He slid his hand in his pocket and pulled out a ring. A platinum eternity band set with blazing canary yellow diamonds, it was jaw-droppingly beautiful.

She lifted her gaze to his, heart thumping in her chest. "A circle of fire," her husband murmured, eyes trained on hers. "What we are, Angelina. What you've always been to me. The woman who gave me my life back…the woman who has given me two beautiful daughters who remind me every day what love is."

Her stomach plunged. *Their anniversary!* She opened her mouth to apologize for forgetting, to tell him how crazy it had been with him away, but her husband shook his head, pressed his fingers to her lips.

"I know how you feel. I've always known how you feel. I want *you* to know what you are to me so there can be no doubt as to how I feel." He pressed her palm to his chest. "This is where you are, *mi amore*. Always here."

A lump in her throat grew until it was too big to get any words around it. She stood on tiptoe and kissed him instead. Passionate, reverential, it spoke of a million forevers.

They danced under the stars then, the party forgotten, a brilliant blanket of light their only witness.

Sometimes you caught the elusive corporate raider.

Sometimes you even captured his heart.

* * * * *

If you enjoyed this book, don't miss Jennifer Hayward's contribution to
THE BILLIONAIRE'S LEGACY *in*
A DEAL FOR THE DI SIONE RING

Also available now is the fabulous
KINGDOMS & CROWNS *trilogy!*
CARRYING THE KING'S PRIDE
CLAIMING THE ROYAL INNOCENT
MARRYING HER ROYAL ENEMY

MILLS & BOON®
Large Print – July 2017

Secrets of a Billionaire's Mistress
Sharon Kendrick

Claimed for the De Carrillo Twins
Abby Green

The Innocent's Secret Baby
Carol Marinelli

The Temporary Mrs Marchetti
Melanie Milburne

A Debt Paid in the Marriage Bed
Jennifer Hayward

The Sicilian's Defiant Virgin
Susan Stephens

Pursued by the Desert Prince
Dani Collins

Return of Her Italian Duke
Rebecca Winters

The Millionaire's Royal Rescue
Jennifer Faye

Proposal for the Wedding Planner
Sophie Pembroke

A Bride for the Brooding Boss
Bella Bucannon